# Blood and Soap

STORIES

**Linh Dinh**

SEVEN STORIES

New York · London · Toronto

Seven Stories Press
140 Watts Street
New York, NY 10013
http://www.sevenstories.com/

In Canada: Hushion House, 36 Northline Road, Toronto, Ontario M4B 3E2

In the UK: Turnaround Publisher Services Ltd., Unit 3, Olympia Trading Estate,
Coburg Road, Wood Green, London N22 6TZ

In Australia: Palgrave Macmillan, 627 Chapel Street, South Yarra VIC 3141

Text design by India Amos

College professors may order examination copies of Seven Stories Press titles
for a free six-month trial period. To order, visit www.sevenstories.com/textbook/
or fax on school letterhead to 212.226.1411.

Library of Congress Cataloging-in-Publication Data

Dinh, Linh, 1963–
 Blood and soap : stories / Linh Dinh.— 1st ed.
    p. cm.
 ISBN 1-58322-642-7 (pbk.)
 1. Vietnam—Social life and customs—Fiction. 2. Vietnamese
Americans—Fiction.  I. Title.
PS3554.I494 B58 2004
813'.6—dc22

                    2003027043

Printed in Canada

# Contents

The following stories have been previously published: "!," "Costa San Giorgio," "13," and "The Self-Portraitist of Signa" in *American Poetry Review*; "Our Newlyweds" and "Prisoner with a Dictionary" in *New American Writing*; "A Floating Community" in *South*; "A Moral Decision" and "Key Words" in the webzine *Tool*; "Eight Plots" in *Interlope*; "One-Sentence Stories" in *Sentence*; "Food Conjuring" in *Michigan Review*; "Parmigiano Cheese" in *Van Gogh's Ear*; and "My Grandfather the Exceptional" in *Tinfish*.

Many of these stories were written while my wife and I were living in Certaldo, Italy, as guests of the town of Certaldo and the International Parliament of Writers. My wife and I would like to thank the IPW and all the citizens of Certaldo for their amazing hospitality—particularly mayor Rosalba Spini and Cristiana Borghini. I'd also like to thank Dan Simon for his friendship and for his steadfast support of my work over the years. Every writer should be this lucky.

# Prisoner with a Dictionary

And so a young man was thrown in prison and found in his otherwise empty cell a foreign dictionary. It was always dark in there and he couldn't even tell that it was a dictionary at first. He was not an intellectual type and had never even owned a dictionary in his life. He was far from stupid, however, but had an ironic turn of mind that could squeeze out a joke from most tragic situations. He could also be very witty around certain women. In any case, he did not know what to do with this nearly worthless book but to use it as a stool and as a pillow. Periodically he also tore out pages from it to wipe himself. Soon, however, out of sheer boredom, he decided to look at this dictionary. His eyes had adjusted to the dim light by now and he could make out all the words with relative ease in that eternal twilight. Although he was not familiar with the foreign language, and did not even know what language it was, he suddenly felt challenged to learn it. His main virtue, and the main curse of his life, was the ability to follow through on any course of action once he had set his mind to it. This book represented the last problem, the only problem, he would ever solve. The prisoner began by picking out words at random and scrutinizing their definitions. Of course, each definition was made up of words entirely unknown to him. Undeterred, he would look up all the words in the definition, which lead him to even more unfathomable words. To define "man," for example, the prisoner had to look up not only "human" and "person" but also "opposable" and "thumb." To define "thumb," he had to look up not only "short" and "digit" but also "thick" and "of" and "a" and "the." To define "the," he had to look up "that" and "a" (again) and "person" (again) and "thing" and "group." Being alone in his cell night and day, without any distraction, allowed the prisoner to concentrate with such rigor that soon he could retain and cross index hundreds of definitions in his head. The dictionary had well over a thousand pages but the prisoner was determined to memorize every definition on every page. He cringed at the thought that he had once torn out pages to wipe himself. These pages now represented to him gaps in his eventual knowledge. Because they were gone forever he would never be able to know *all* the words in that particular language. Still, it was with an elation bordering on madness that he woke up each morning, eager to eat up more words. Like many people, he equated the acquisition of a vast vocabulary with knowledge, even with wisdom, and so he could feel his stature growing by the day, if not by the second. Although he did not know what the words meant, what they referred to in real life, he reasoned that he *understood* these words because he knew their definitions. And because he was living inside this language all the time, like a fetus thriving inside a womb, there were times when he felt sure he could guess at the general implications of a word, whether it was a plant or an animal, for example, or whether it indicated something positive or negative. But his guesses were always wrong, of course. Because "bladder" sounded somehow vast and nebulous to the prisoner, he thought that it must have something to do with the outdoors, most likely the weather, a gust of wind or a torrential rain or a bolt of lightning. "Father," with its forlorn, exasperated tone, made the prisoner think of something dead and putrid: a corpse or a heap of garbage. He guessed that "homicide" was a flower. He thought "July" meant "August." The prisoner was also justifiably proud of his pronunciation, which was remarkably crisp and confident, the stresses more often than not falling on the right syllables. If he were to speak on the phone, the prisoner could almost be mistaken for a native speaker, albeit one of the lower class. But if the prisoner was convinced he was gaining a new language he was also surely losing one because he had, by this time, forgotten nearly all the words of his native language. By this time he could no longer name any part of the anatomy, even the most basic, hand, nose, face, mouth, etc., and so his own body was becoming vague, impersonal, unreal. Although he was surrounded by filth, he could no longer conjure up the word "filth." The only word that came readily to his tongue, automatically, unbidden, was "prison" because that was the last thing he thought of each night, and the first thing he thought of each morning. His dreams had become entirely devoid of conversations or thoughts. Often they were just a series of images or abstract patches of colors. Sometimes they were also made up entirely of sounds, a cacophony of his own voice reciting bits of definitions. Even in his worst nightmare, he could no longer shout out "mother!" in his own language. But this loss never bothered him, he barely noticed it, because he was convinced he was remaking himself anew. As he was being squeezed out of the world, the only world he had a right to belong in, he thought he was entering a new universe. Perhaps by purging himself of his native language, the prisoner was unconsciously trying to get rid of his horrible past, because, frankly, there was not a single word of his native tongue that did not evoke, for the prisoner, some horrible experience or humiliation. Perhaps he could sense that his native tongue was the very *author* of his horrible life. But these are only conjectures, we do not know for sure. In any case nights and days the prisoner shouted out definitions to himself. If one were to press one's ear against the thick iron door at midnight, one would hear, for example: "an animal with a long, thin tail that commonly infests buildings." Or "a deep and tender feeling for an arch enemy." Or "a shuddering fear and disgust accompanied by much self loathing." With so many strange words and definitions accumulating, surely some profound knowledge, some revelation, was at hand? What is a revelation, after all, but the hard-earned result of an exceptional mind working at peak capacity? The prisoner was thankful to be given a chance to concentrate unmolested for such a continuous length of time. He felt himself victorious: condemned to an empty cell, he had been robbed of the world, but through a heroic act of will, he had remade the universe. He had (nearly) everything because he had (nearly) all the words of an entire language. But the truth is the prisoner had regained nothing. He only thought that way, of course, because he had to think that way. After decades of unceasing mental exertion, the only fruit of the prisoner's remarkable labor, the only word he ever acquired for sure, was "dictionary," simply because it was printed on the cover of a book he knew for sure was a dictionary. For even as he ran across the definition for "prisoner," and was memorizing it by heart, he didn't even know that he was only reading about himself.

# Our Northernmost Governor

If it's true that each country is reflected by its government, then we must be the most dishonest and idiotic people in the world. In any case, we are the most superstitious. Like savages or schizophrenics, we see signs everywhere. We believe the universe is a web of causes and effects decipherable through magic and intuition. If eleven clouds were aligned in the sky and our soccer team won a match, for example, then these two extremely rare phenomena had to be related. We distrust all sciences.

As a rational man, a lawyer and a disciple of Cicero, however, I can step away from the common stupidities of my fellow countrymen. I don't believe you must squash the head of a snake when you kill it to prevent it from biting you three days later. Nor do I believe that buttons must be removed from the shirt of a corpse to allow it to reach the afterlife. Nor do I believe that oral sex erases short-term memories. (Our prostitutes don't mind "playing jazz," it is said, because they want their short-term memories erased.) But a man cannot divorce himself from the ethos of his homeland completely. I've had a few incidents in my life that can only be deemed miraculous. I'll give you just one example. This happened nine years ago:

I had just finished a meal at Fang's, a Chinese restaurant downtown, when I opened a newspaper to see my father's face smiling at me. Dressed in a badly cut suit, he was about to cut the ribbon at some ceremony. A glance at the caption revealed the man to be the governor of our northernmost province. Still, his resemblance to my father was so uncanny that I decided to cut the image out to show it to him later that evening. This act became so imperative that I demanded, in a very gruff voice, that the waiter brought me a pair of scissors immediately.

The governor's face resembled my father's in every detail, down to the chipped tooth and misaligned eyebrows. He even wore my father's favorite paisley tie. We'll have a good laugh over this, I thought as I waited impatiently for the waiter to return with a pair of scissors.

Although my father and I did not always enjoy the warmest relationship, we did get along and we did love each other. As he grew more dependent on me, I became more tolerant of him. I gradually learnt to forgive all the cruelties he had inflicted on us when the old man was the man of the house. How he had forced his wife and five children to be vegetarians until, literally overnight, he decided to become a meat eater. After that we were made to eat pork almost every night. He did not let me date a girl until I was twenty-one. I even learnt to forget the fact that he had kept many mistresses, a situation that humiliated my mother when she was alive.

My father also crammed us constantly with a million tidbits of useless information. At every family gathering, he would blurt out weird sentences such as: "Do you know that Leonard da Vinci wrote backward?" Or: "An elephant hair can be used as a toothpick!" Or: "If a panda gives birth to twins, she would only raise one, and left the other to die!" Or: "The flags of Monaco and Indonesia are exactly the same!" He simply assumed that anything he happened to know or cared about was relevant to everyone else's well-being, but perhaps

that's not such an unusual presumption.

But, like I said, we did get along and we did love each other. We had several interests in common. We were both soccer fanatics and went to the stadium for every important match. My father was something of a wordsmith and came up with many memorable phrases to describe his favorite players. A midfielder was said to have "the dreamlike tenacity of a marathon runner." He praised our national goalie for having "the grunting concentration of a weightlifter." As for the opposing team, he loved to throw batteries at them.

We also enjoyed an occasional game of chess and a snifter or two of cognac in the evening.

What we did not have in common was any physical resemblance. A few relatives even suspected I was a bastard. A ridiculous rumor. My mother was absolutely faithful.

When the waiter returned with the scissors, I grabbed them eagerly from his hand. To my chagrin, the young man did not go away but stood where he was to watch me cut the image out. He even asked me impudently, "Someone you know, Sir?"

Maybe it was because I was being observed, but my hand trembled as I clipped. I felt light-headed and my eyes blurred. The waiter seemed to enjoy my nervousness and even started to whistle. As soon as I finished, I realized what I had done: by cutting my father's likeness out of the newspaper, I had removed him from the world. I had just committed patricide. The waiter snatched the scissors from my hand and walked briskly away. I thought for a moment he was going to call the police. Sure enough, when I returned home, I found the old man lying dead on the sofa.

The coroner fixed the time of death between five and six o'clock, the exact time I spent at the restaurant. I knew in my heart I was a murderer. For years afterwards, I had a recurring nightmare of being strapped to an electric chair. I also had dreams of my father walking through a revolving door or sitting in an airport lounge, smoking a cigar. But how could I resist cutting his image out of the newspaper when the man in the photo had suggested it to me himself by holding a pair of scissors in his hand?

In my desperation to cast off guilt, I came up with an alternative explanation: since a man cannot be in two places at the same time, my father had to die before I showed him the photo. Conversely, if I had intended to show the governor a photo of my father, then the governor would have died.

I decided, finally, that my father's death was not so much a murder but a suicide, or at least an assisted suicide. Bored, constantly drunk, and in poor health, he wanted his life to end but he did not have the courage to kill himself. He needed me to help him. Since he could not ask me directly, he caused the photo of our northernmost governor to appear in the newspaper to entice me into killing him.

In *The Workers* newspaper of October 10, 2000, there was a curious item about a fake doctor. A certain Ngo Thi Nghe had been practicing medicine for over ten years on a false degree, which she procured, it is speculated, by killing its original owner. She had all the accoutrements of medicine, a white suit, a thermometer, a bedpan, a syringe, many bottles of pills, but no formal knowledge of medicine. In fact, she had never gotten out of the eighth grade. The mortality rate of her patients, however, was no higher than usual, and she was even defended by some of her clients, after all the facts had come out, for saving their lives. "A most compassionate doctor," said one elderly gentleman.

There are so many scams nowadays that this case drew no special attention. Every day there are news reports of fake lawyers, fake architects, fake professors, and fake politicians doing business without the proper license or training. A most curious case in recent memory, however, is that of Ho Muoi, who was accused of being a fake English teacher. From perusing innumerable newspaper accounts, I was able to piece together the following:

Ho Muoi was born in 1952 in Ky Dong village. His family made firecrackers until they were banned because of the war. Thereafter the father became an alcoholic and left the family. Although Ho Muoi was only six at the time, he knew enough to swear that he would never mention or even think of his father's name again. His mother supported the children, all five of them, by carrying water and night soil for hire, a backbreaking labor that made her shorter by several inches. She also made meat dumplings that she sold on special occasions.

Ky Dong Village is known for a festival, held every January 5th, in honor of a legendary general of a mythical king who fought against a real enemy two or three thousand years ago. The festival features a duck-catching demonstration, a wrestling tournament for the boys, a meat dumpling making contest for the girls, and, until it was banned because of the war, a procession of firecrackers.

Those who've witnessed this procession of firecrackers describe a scene where boys and girls and gay men jiggle papier-mâché animals and genitals strung from bamboo sticks amid the smoke and din of a million firecrackers.

But the excitement from the festival only came once a year. For the rest of the time, the villagers were preoccupied with the tedium and anxieties of daily life. Most of the young men were drafted into the army, sent away and never came back, but the war never came directly to Ky Dong Village.

When Ho Muoi was ten, his mother enrolled him in school for the first time. He was slow and it took him a year to learn the alphabet. He could never figure out how to add or subtract. His worst subject, however, was geography. It was inconceivable to him that there are hundreds of countries in the world, each with a different spoken language. Every single word of his own language felt so inevitable that he thought it would be a crime against nature to call a cow or a bird anything different.

Ho Muoi could not even conceive of *two* countries sharing this same earth. "Countries" in the plural sounds like either a tautology or an oxymoron. "Country," "earth," and "universe" were all synonymous in his mind.

Ho Muoi's teacher was a very sophisticated young man from Hanoi. He was the only one within a fifty-mile radius who had ever read a newspaper or who owned even a single book. He even fancied himself a poet in his spare time. He did not mind teaching a bunch of village idiots, however, because it spared him from the bombs and landmines that were the fate of his contemporaries. In the evening he could be found in his dark room reading a Russian novel. The teacher was short and scrawny and had a habit of shutting his eyes tight and sticking his lips out when concentrating. Still, it was odd that he managed to attract no women in a village almost entirely emptied of its young men.

Whenever this teacher was exasperated with his charge he would shout "!" but no one knew what the word meant or what language it was in so it was dismissed as a sort of a sneeze or a clearing of the throat.

At twelve, something happened to Ho Muoi that would change his whole outlook on life. He was walking home from school when he saw a crowd gathering around three men who were at least two heads taller than the average person. The men had a pink, almost red complexion and their hair varied from a bright orange to a whitish yellow. They were not unfriendly and allowed people to tug at the abundant hair growing on their arms. "Wonderful creatures," Ho Muoi thought as

" ! "

he stared at them, transfixed. One of the men noticed Ho Muoi and started to say something. The words were rapid, like curses, but the man was smiling as he was saying them. All eyes turned to look at Ho Muoi. Some people started to laugh and he wanted to laugh along with them but he could not. Suddenly his face flushed and he felt an intense hatred against these foreign men. If he had a gun he would have shot them already. Without premeditation he blurted out "!" then ran away.

When Ho Muoi got home his heart was still beating wildly. The excitement of blurting out a magical word, a word he did not know the meaning of, was overwhelming. He also remembered the look of shock on the man's face after the word had left his mouth. He repeated "!" several times and felt its power each time.

Ho Muoi would think about this incident for years afterward. He recalled how he was initially enraged by a series of foreign words, and that he had retaliated with a foreign word of his own. In his mind, foreign words became equated with a terrible power. The fact that his own language would be foreign to a foreigner never occurred to him.

The incident also turned Ho Muoi into a celebrity. The villagers would recall with relish how one of their own, a twelve-year-old boy, had "stood up to a foreigner" by hurling a curse at him in his own language. Many marveled at the boy's intelligence for knowing how to use a foreign word, heard maybe once or twice in passing, on just the right occasion and with authority. They even suggested to the schoolteacher that he teach "the boy genius" all the foreign words from his Russian novels.

The schoolteacher never got around to doing this. He was drafted soon after, sent south, and was never heard from again. As for Ho Muoi, he became convinced that, given the opportunity, he could quickly learn any foreign language. This opportunity came after Ho Muoi himself was drafted into the army.

His battalion served in the Central Highlands, along the Truong Son Mountain, guarding supply lines. They rarely made contact with the enemy but whenever they did, Ho Muoi acquitted himself miserably. He often froze and had to be literally kicked into action. What was perceived by his comrades as cowardice, however, was not so much a fear of physical pain as the dread that he would not be allowed to fulfill his destiny.

The war was an outrage, Ho Muoi thought, not because it was wiping out thousands of people a day, the young, the old, and the unborn, but that it could exterminate a man of destiny like himself. And yet he understood that wars also provide many lessons to those who survived them. A war is a working man's university. Knowing that, he almost felt grateful.

Ho Muoi also had the superstition (or the inspiration) that if the war eliminates a single book from this earth, then that would be a greater loss than all the lives wasted. The death of a man affects three or four other individuals, at most. Its significance is symbolic and sentimental, but the loss of a single book is tangible, a disaster which should be mourned forever by all of mankind. The worth of a society is measured by how many books it has produced. This, from a man who had never actually read a book. Ho Muoi had seen so few books, he could not tell one from another; they were all equal in his mind. He never suspected that war is the chief generator of books. A war is a thinking man's university.

In 1970 or 1971, after a brief skirmish, they caught an American soldier whom they kept for about thirty days. The prisoner was made to march along with Ho Muoi's battalion until he fell ill and died (he was not badly injured). This man was given the same ration as the others but the food did not agree with him. Once, they even gave him an extra helping of orangutan meat, thinking it would restore his health.

As the prisoner sank into delirium, the color drained from his face but his eyes lit up. He would blather for hours on end. No one paid him any attention but Ho Muoi. In his tiny notebook he would record as much of the man's rambling as possible. These phonetic notations became the source for Ho Muoi's English lessons after the war. I've seen pages from the notebook. Its lines often ran diagonally from one corner to another. A typical run-on sentence: "hoo he hoo ah utta ma nut m pap m home."

The notebook also includes numerous sketches of the American. Each portrait was meant as a visual clue to the words swarming around it. Ho Muoi's skills as an artist were so poor, however, that the face depicted always appeared the same, that of a young man, any man, really, who has lost all touch with the world.

Ho Muoi was hoping his unit would catch at least one more American so he could continue his English lesson, but this tutor never materialized, unfortunately.

Though all the English he had was contained within a single notebook, Ho Muoi was not discouraged. The American must have spoken just about every word there was in his native language, he reasoned, through all those nights of raving. And the invisible words can be inferred from the visible ones.

Words are like numbers, he further reasoned, a closed system with a small set of self-generated rules. And words arranged on a page resemble a dull, monotonous painting. If one could look at the weirdest picture and decipher, sooner or later, its organizing principle, why can't one do the same with words?

"!"

Everything seems chaotic at first, but nothing is chaotic. One can read anything: ants crawling on the ground; pimples on a face; trees in a forest. Fools will argue with you about this, but any surface can be deciphered. The entire world, as seen from an airplane, is just a warped surface.

A man may fancy he's making an abstract painting, but there is no such thing as an abstract painting, only abstracted ones. Every horizontal surface is a landscape because it features a horizon (thus implying a journey, escape from the self, and the unreachable). Every vertical surface is either a door or a portrait (thus implying a house, another being, yourself as another being, and the unreachable). And all colors have shared and private associations. Red may inspire horror in one culture, elation in another, but it is still red, is still blood. Green always evokes trees and a pretty green dress.

Ho Muoi also believed that anything made by man can be duplicated: a chair, a gun, a language, provided one has the raw materials, as he did, with his one notebook of phonetic notations. If one can break apart a clock and reassemble it, one can scramble up phonetic notations and rearrange them in newer combinations, thus ending up with not just a language, but a literature.

At the time of his arrest, Ho Muoi was teaching hundreds of students beginning, intermediate, and advanced English three nights a week. For twenty-five years, he had taught his students millions of vocabulary words. He had patiently explained to them the intricacies of English grammar, complete with built-in inconsistencies. He had even given them English poems and short stories (written by himself and the more advanced students) to read. When interrogated at the police station, however, our English teacher proved ignorant of the most basic knowledge of the language. He did not know the verb "to be" or "to do." He did not know there is a past tense in English. He had never heard of Shakespeare and was not even aware that Australians and Englishmen also speak English.

In Ho Muoi's made-up English, there are not five but twenty-four vowels. The new nuances in pronunciation force each student to fine-tune his ear to the level of the finest musician. There is a vast vocabulary for pain and bamboo but no equivalent for cheese. Any adjective can be used as a verb. *I will hot you*, for example, or, *Don't red me*. There are so many personal pronouns, each one denoting an exact relationship between speaker and subject, that even the most brilliant student cannot master them all.

By sheer coincidence, some of Ho Muoi's made-up English words correspond exactly with actual English. In his system, a cat is also called a cat; a tractor, a tractor; and a rose, inevitably, perhaps, a rose.

Some of his more curious inventions include *blanket*, to denote a husband. *Basin*, to denote a wife. *Pin prick*: a son. *A leaky faucet*: a daughter.

Ho Muoi's delusion was so absolute, however, that after he was sentenced to twenty-five years for "defrauding the people," he asked to be allowed to take to prison a "Dictionary of the English Language" and a "Dictionary of English Slang," two volumes he himself had compiled, so that "I can continue my life studies."

It is rumored that many of his former students have banded together to continue their English lessons. Harassed by the police, they must hold their nightly meetings in underground bunkers, lit by oil lamps. Their strange syllables, carried by the erratic winds, crosshatch the surrounding countryside.

But why are they doing this? You ask. Don't they know they are studying a false language?

As the universal language—for now—English represents to these students the rest of the world. English *is* the world. These students also know that Vietnam, as it exists, is not of this world. To cling even to a false English is to insist on another reality.

A bogus English is better than no English, is better, in fact, than actual English, since it corresponds to no English or American reality.

Hoo he hoo ah utta ma nut m pap m home.

The Red River Delta is one of the most populated areas on earth: for hundreds of square miles, there are village after village, town after town, and each available (and unavailable) acre of land is cultivated. That's why Noi Yen is such an anomaly. Located in the heart of the Red River Delta, a mere fifty miles from Hanoi, the town is almost completely abandoned. I've only seen it once, in September or October of 1998, and I don't think I'd ever want to see it again.

Arriving from busy, thriving Hung Chan, crossing a stinking, narrow creek, I was first startled by the empty, ghostly aspect of Noi Yen's main street. All of its houses and shops were shuttered. Many appeared vandalized and had fallen into ruins, uninhabited, an unheard of phenomenon in Vietnam, where even concrete pillboxes from the French era, built more than half a century ago, are converted into dwellings. About the only life in Noi Yen's "commercial district" were a dozen beggars and hawkers, selling almost nothing, who gathered in the blue shadow of the eternally closed post office. One of them, a ten-year-old girl, tried to run after our car waving a fistful of lottery tickets. We left her standing in the dust.

Leaving the town itself, I was further shocked by the sights of the deserted countryside. For many miles I did not see a single buffalo, chicken, dog, or bird. All the fields lay fallow, overgrown with weeds and wild flowers, and every few feet there was a small, carelessly dug pit. There were literally hundreds of these pits. "Was there a battle here?" I asked my driver, rather stupidly, as it turned out, as I'd never seen a real battlefield in my life. "No," he answered me tersely, and stepped on the gas pedal to speed us away. Sensing my annoyance, he quickly added: "I'll tell you all about Noi Yen once we get to the next town."

Later, over dinner and a dozen bottles of Hanoi beer, he finally explained: "Noi Yen has been abandoned for about ten years now. No one can live there, it is cursed. There are a handful of explanations, but the most convincing, and therefore it must be true, is the story of the empty coffin."

"The empty coffin?!"

"Yes, the empty coffin. You see, about fifteen years ago, there was a feud between Noi Yen and Hung Chan, and the people of Hung Chan put a curse on Noi Yen, and that's why no one can live there any more."

"What was the feud over?"

"I'm not sure, but I think it was because some men from Hung Chan had raped a girl from Hung Chan, or maybe somebody had insulted somebody, or maybe somebody owed somebody money and didn't want to pay, or maybe it was because Noi Yen had beaten Hung Chan in a soccer match by bribing the referee."

The vagueness of the origin of the feud annoyed me a little, but then I thought it really doesn't matter, since there are so many reasons, all valid, of course, human beings may decide to exact revenge on each another.

My driver continued: "You see, once the feud between the two towns had started, there was a rash of strange deaths in Noi Yen. People would simply drop dead as they were going about their daily business. I could be sitting in a café talking to you, as I'm doing now, and without warnings, I would crash to the ground and be dead within a few seconds."

"How many strange deaths were there altogether?"

"Hundreds!"

I squinted at my driver skeptically. Four or five heart attacks at most, or maybe epileptic fits, or cases of food poisoning. Why do we always exaggerate so much, my friend?

Talking of food poisoning, I remember that what we had that night was truly awful. We had asked for different varieties of noodle soups, mine with seafood, his with chicken, but the waitress only smiled at us most pleasantly, then went into the kitchen to return a minute later with two bowls of identical slop, both with thin strips of old pork in them. That's what can happen when you travel to these forsaken towns: you are either pleasantly surprised by a local delicacy at a giveaway price, or they make you pay through the nose for garbage.

My driver chugged down his mug of beer, spilling plenty out of the sides of his mouth, then continued: "Yes, there were hundreds of deaths within a month, each day there were at least a dozen funerals, but no one could prove that these strange deaths were caused by a curse from Hung Chan. But there were no other valid explanations! Before the feud, no one was dying!"

My driver paused to grope into the ice bucket for yet another bottle of beer, his eighth or ninth, then continued: "So it was clear there was a curse, but since no one in Noi Yen knew what that curse was, they could not neutralize it. But then, out of pity, perhaps, someone from Hung Chan finally let on that there was an empty coffin buried in Noi Yen. That's why so many people were dying. The coffin needed a corpse, and until there was a real corpse placed inside it, the people of Noi Yen would continue to drop dead."

"And that's why there were all those pits in the fields?"

"Yes, yes, the people of Noi Yen knew there was an empty coffin buried in their town, but they did not know exactly where it was, and that's why they had to dig all over, just so they could place a corpse inside it."

His reasoning *does* make some sense, I thought. Everyone knows that when coffin sales are going slow, coffin makers like to sleep inside a coffin to suggest death to the gods, to induce business. It is also self-evident that a coffin above ground is just a coffin, but a coffin underground *must* have a body inside it.

"And they never found the coffin?"

"Of course not. That's why they had to flee the town. In their desperation the people of Noi Yen had even hired a famous Buddhist monk from Hanoi to locate the coffin, but even this monk couldn't find it. The monk claimed the coffin was eluding him."

"What do you mean 'eluding him'?!"

"The coffin was moving around underground to escape detection!"

"But I thought the coffin wanted to be detected, so it could have a body inside it."

My driver remained silent for a few seconds. I had finally stumped him, I thought. But then he said: "You see, a coffin is not unlike a woman. It wants a body, but it acts as if it doesn't really want a body. It doesn't want to be pregnant!"

"Is that what the famous monk said?!"

"No, monks don't know anything about women. But it makes common sense. It's what I'm telling you."

Yes, a female coffin, made of cheap wood surely, homely, secretly and hastily inserted into the ground, eternally hankering for the chilled body of any man, woman, or child, but resisting the paid susurration of a fake monk.

"But maybe there's simply no empty coffin in the ground?"

"But of course there is. That's why all those people were dying."

"But not everyone fled. We saw a dozen people today, by the post office. How come they're not dropping dead?"

My driver looked at me with blood shot eyes. He was completely drunk by now and would probably crash into the first truck or tree we saw after we got back into the car. I had known he was a lush before I hired him but his vehicle, an old Soviet junker, could be had for dirt cheap. It appeared we would have to jostle for a place inside the empty coffin that night.

"I saw no one in Noi Yen today, Sir. Even a dog would be afraid to live in that cursed town. The people who have moved away don't even dare to come back for half a day to tend to their relatives' graves. If you saw a dozen people today then they had to be ghosts. What were they doing?"

"They were begging and selling trinkets."

"That just proves it. They had to be ghosts because no one is crazy enough to go to a ghost town to beg or to sell trinkets."

# Those Who Are No Longer with Us

Hotel rooms are like airport bars: devoid of personal history, falsely intimate, and vaguely promising. The first night in a hotel room is always exhilarating because one has just escaped from home. The last night is also (similarly) exhilarating because one is about to go home. Asides from the basics, a comfortable bed, a flushing toilet, one also chooses a hotel for its breathtaking or eccentric looking lobby, a transporting view from one's window, and a restaurant serving dishes that are neither cosmopolitan nor local but truly out of this world. Hotels to be avoided are the ones with a snoring receptionist, a stuck elevator, bedbugs, centipedes, ghosts, and tricks.

While a snoring receptionist can be readily spotted upon entering the lobby, one does not know that one has checked into a haunted hotel until it is too late. Alas, the percentage of hotel rooms in our country frequented by those who are no longer with us is not high. Out of more than 250,000 rooms, no more than 500, at most, are haunted. I have traveled up and down this great, tiny country of ours and have unavoidably (and unequivocally) spent a few nights in haunted hotel rooms. While these experiences were unnerving enough at the time, they have caused me no permanent psychological or physical injuries.

My first experience with a hotel ghost was benign enough. While staying in the penthouse suite at one of the biggest and most expensive hotels in Hanoi, I was tickled all night by a ghost. As soon as I was about to sleep, somebody would tickle my feet. When I complained to management in the morning, they gave me a full refund, surprisingly enough. They did ask me, however, to never mention the name of their hotel in talking about this incident. (They even offered me cash to claim that I had stayed at a rival hotel.) This hotel, built at enormous cost, was then operating only at a quarter-occupancy. The last thing they wanted was public knowledge that it was haunted. A child had fallen down the dumbwaiter several years ago. Every so often it would return to tickle the feet of hotel guests.

My second experience with a hotel ghost took place in Pleiku. Why would anyone want to go to Pleiku? It is precisely because there is no reason to go there that I went there. Every place on this earth is worth visiting at least once, I believe. After spending the day looking at the wonderfully nondescript Catholic church, a similarly undistinguished Buddhist temple, and the mausoleum-like post office, I retreated to my room in the Hollywood Hotel. A perfunctory scan of the four TV stations yielded the same program, a report on the Party Congress in Hanoi, and so I decided to call it an early night. I was eager to get out of town the next morning, satisfied that I'd "done Pleiku."

Around three in the morning I was startled awake by the din of rock music. Though I'm no fan of American pop culture, I'm familiar enough with it to recognize the screaming vocals of Joe Cocker. Must be one of those backpackers, I thought. The volume was so loud it sounded like a live concert in my room. After Joe Cocker, Janis Joplin came on. Then Jimi Hendrix. Then the Jefferson Airplane. In short, it was Woodstock, but in the middle of the Vietnamese hinterland. Why is no one complaining? And why does the management tolerate such a disturbance? We need tourist money, certainly, but not this kind of tourists. I decided to take matters into my own hand. I got dressed quickly and went to open the door, only to discover that it was locked! In my fury I alternated between kicking the door and yanking the doorknob. This went on for several minutes until the nearly splintered door finally swung open. The music had suddenly stopped. In the hallway were several of the hotel staff. The angry and shocked looks on their faces showed that they were staring at a madman.

No, no one has heard loud music, rock or otherwise. The backpackers are very well behaved and in their room. It is you, Sir, who are not maintaining the standards of Socialist behavior. And who, by the way, is Jimi Hendrix?

My third experience with a hotel ghost took place in Vinh and was also auditory. I had gone there to inspect its famous walking tree. This mango tree is reputedly a thousand years old. One of its branches has sagged to the ground, taken roots, and became a new trunk. The old trunk withered away over time. In a thousand years it has thus "walked" about three feet.

After having a Polaroid taken in front of the walking tree, I strolled about town, discovered nothing, and retreated to my room in the North Star Oasis, a very modern hotel built like a cruise ship lying on its side.

It was not yet dusk and I had only intended to lie down for an hour or so before going back out to dinner. I wanted to sample barbecued field rats, a local delicacy. The town even had a temple dedicated to a particularly large rodent caught more than a century ago. In my sleep someone called my name and I opened my eyes to a darkened room. I had no idea where I was and blurted out, Where am I? A sexless voice answered, But you're here, of course. For some reason this answer saddened me immeasurably. I had even started to sob when the light flicked on by itself, snapping me out of my trance.

The nightstand reassured me. The room was as it was, with a small TV on top of a small refrigerator. On the wall was a calendar showing a lakeside castle in Switzerland.

(The calendar was a year old, incidentally. When I asked about this, I was told that it was the manager's idea, "so that each guest would feel a year younger.")

My fourth and last experience with a hotel ghost was both auditory and tactile. I am an aficionado of buffalo fights and will travel a thousand miles to see two large beasts lunge at each other to the death. (Cockfights are for pansies living in small apartments.) Real men go for real beasts. On this occasion I was in Thi Cau Village for its annual buffalo fight. The festivities were capped off by a seven-course feast of buffalo meat. Drunk and happy, I retreated to the only public accommodation in town, a miserable ten-room guesthouse across the street from a bumpy soccer field. The bed was sagging and promised a sore back in the morning.

In the dark, I thought about the special place the buffalo has in our hearts. We talk to him as a friend and compose hundreds of poems about him. We love the buffalo so much that we continue to employ him when farmers in every other country have long moved on to tractors. My reverie was disturbed by three faint knocks on the door. It was already past midnight. I shouted, "Who is it?!" No one answered. Maybe it was because of the alcohol but I felt unusually belligerent.

Who's this asshole knocking on my door in the middle of the night? Suddenly it occurred to me that it was probably only a prostitute. The receptionist had likely alerted her to the fact that there was a single male staying at the guesthouse that night. In centuries past, many of the king's concubines came from Thi Cau Village.

But I was not a king, of course, and, furthermore, I had reached a point in life when memories of sex often prove much more exciting than sex itself. On the other hand, I thought, this is such an unusually poor village. If I could contribute to the local economy in any way . . . The knocks came again, as faint as the first time. Still undecided about what to do with one-of-those-who-sells-flowers-by-night on the other side of the door, I nevertheless went to open it.

They say that when there's a ghost in the vicinity the temperature will drop and there will be a faint, foul odor. When I opened the door I was greeted by a rotten smell and a gust of cold wind, like a blast from an air conditioner. I stepped into the hallway to look around. At one end of the dim hallway was a broom and a plastic trash can; at the other end was a mural of Uncle Ho giving a girl, a pioneer youth, a bag of lollipops. There was no one around. I must admit to a feeling of disappointment as I closed the door and returned to bed.

Now that my musing on the buffalo had been interrupted, I could think of nothing else but what had been promised me a moment earlier. To get it over with, I could evoke one (or several) of the few amorous episodes from my long life worth reminiscing about. I noticed that the rotten smell had entered the room and that it had gotten considerably colder. I pulled the blanket to my chin and conjured up my first girlfriend, a high school classmate who liked to baby talk, then the older woman who introduced me to mud and yogurt, then the girl who always asked, Am I hurting you? as she bounced up and down. As I hearten to these memories, I became conscious of another presence lying under the blanket. Maybe it was because I was drunk, but I chose to ignore it to continue with my roll call of girlfriends.

When something happens in the dark you can almost pretend it is not happening at all. Not this, however. Whatever it was that was under the blanket with me suddenly started to embrace me from all sides. I was engulfed by it. Every inch of my body was pressed against another's flesh. No matter how I twisted and turned this point-for-point contact continued. This other flesh was not warm, however, but cold, and had no anatomy. There were no arms, legs, stomach, or breasts. The foul smell also intensified, becoming nearly insufferable. Though my senses were completely overwhelmed I was, how shall I put it, not displeased. A moment after our struggle had reached its climax, I was left alone again.

I had gotten what I had asked for, I suppose. I felt spent, emptied of myself. The room was moonlit and I could hear crickets and bull-frogs through the open window. I closed my eyes but did not sleep for the rest of the night. This episode would be added to my selected list of erotic adventures, to be relived time and again in other hotel rooms.

# Our Newlyweds

The wedding began at Notre Dame Cathedral and ended at the Majestic
Hotel. Although hardly the most beautiful church in Saigon, Notre
Dame is its most famous. Built in 1877 in a neo-Romanesque style,
the cathedral's twin towers lord over one end of Dong Khoi Street
(previously known as Tu Do Street and Rue Catinat). At the other end
of the mile-long street, sloping gently towards the stinking waters of
the Saigon River, is the Majestic Hotel.

The Majestic Hotel was built in 1925 by a Vietnamese-Chinese
known as Uncle Hoa. A real estate magnate, he inspired one half of
a popular jingle: "Ride Uncle Hy's train, live on Uncle Hoa's street."
The hotel has changed names several times. At one point, it was called
the Rising Dragon Hotel.

Halfway between the Majestic Hotel and Notre Dame Cathedral is
the world-famous Continental. Built in 1880, it has a prominent role
in at least two decent novels. Pressing your nose against one of its plate
glass windows, you will see a carved elephant the size of a bear and
dark wooden chairs on a marble floor beneath a crystal chandelier.

The Continental's receptionist is thirty-five. He speaks a casual
English, a coy French, and a flippant Chinese.

Under the neon-haloed Jesus, they held each other's hands. As
friends and family looked on, they pledged to remain together until
death. He was wearing a black suit rented for thirty bucks from a
shop in Cho Lon. Though experienced, the bride was resplendent in

a white dress. To escape the heat, some of the guests were standing in the street.

The priest was exhausted after presiding over his third wedding in two days. Holding a microphone in his right hand, he declared: "The true art of married life, mumble, mumble, mumble, a mutual enrichment, mumble, mumble, mumble, a mingling of two, mumble, mumble, mumble, which diminishes, mumble, mumble, mumble, not a destination, mumble, mumble, mumble, but a journey."

The park outside the church is a gathering place for dating couples. They sit at little folding tables to drink root beer and to munch on dried squid. In the middle of the park is a white statue of the Virgin Mary. In her cupped hands is a globe with a cross sticking out of it.

Our newlyweds emerged into the sunlight of their married life and entered a flower-bedecked white limousine. The car circled the park once then rolled down Dong Khoi Street.

It sped past Spago, Givral, Brodard, and the Paloma Café. Clutching the groom's hand, the bride evoked, once again, the time they went to Brodard to listen to music. They had just met then. The pianist and guitarist were virtuosos. Unmentioned was a brief spat over the groom's gushing praise of a female torch singer.

Dong Khoi Street is shaded mostly by tamarinds and bougainvillea. The often-misspelled bougainvillea is a woody tropical vine of the four-o'clock family. The tamarind is a leguminous tree. Its sour fruit can be eaten raw or candied.

A sign of the decline of Dong Khoi Street are the many galleries selling kitsch. Wildly popular among tourists are reproductions of van Gogh, Botero, and Renoir. These are cranked out effortlessly in backrooms by whiskered, bereted, and protein-deficient artisans, each with a framed certificate from the National Academy of Fine Arts.

Only ten tables were reserved at the Majestic for the reception. Extortionate cost had forced our newlyweds to trim their guest list. They were prohibited from inviting, in the groom's words: "all the riffraff of our extended families."

Guests were treated to white seaweed with crabmeat soup, jellyfish with shredded chicken salad, beef kebab with rice vermicelli, roasted duck in tamarind sauce, and, finally, fried rice with asparagus and ham.

The wedding cake had five tiers, with green garlands and purple flowers spiraling toward a gazebo at the top enclosing a dancing couple.

Food at a wedding often disappoints, while food at a funeral is better than expected. Perhaps eating in the proximity of a coffin makes one better appreciate the simple acts of opening one's mouth, biting, chewing, and swallowing. At a wedding, the obligation to share in someone else's supposed happiness makes all private indulgence impossible.

The soft drinks were free but alcohol cost extra. To save a few bucks, our newlyweds shunned the traditional champagne for bottles of snake wine and Hanoi Vodka.

Snake wine is basically rice wine with a snake, pickled white, coiled up in it. It is believed by the simple-minded, the vain, and the feeble to be an aphrodisiac. "For your wedding night!" the groom's best friend roared as all the men and half the women raised their champagne glasses containing snake wine. When the snake wine ran out everyone switched to Hanoi Vodka.

Hanoi Vodka is the drink of choice for indigent hicks on special occasions. "Clear hell in a bottle," they call it. Although neither the groom nor the bride was an indigent hick, they both liked to weave rustic touches into their lives.

Some blamed what happened later on the snake wine. Others on the Hanoi Vodka. Perhaps it was a combination of both.

A childhood friend of the bride, who gave her her first kiss at fourteen, stood up and dedicated this poem to the newlyweds:

> The robin eats longans.
> The fighting fish knows its tub.
> Husband and wife are familiar
> With each other's smell.

Two or three people clapped. The bride smiled. The groom smirked. The rest weren't paying attention.

The wedding is the culmination of youth, a fulfillment of its aim. It is a public disavowal of selfishness. The true consummation of the wedding is the birth of the first child.

There are two banquet rooms available in the five-story Majestic. (With its tall ceilings, each story really equals two.) One is called Prima; the other, Serenade. Serenade is located on the roof, adjacent to the Breeze Sky Bar. Our wedding reception took place in Serenade.

The Majestic's rooftop veranda is its top attraction as a banquet facility. Guests have ample room to stroll around with a drink in hand to gaze at the nearby skyscrapers, the river, and the clear night sky. The noise, the stench, and the congestion of the city seem very far away.

A hydrofoil on the Saigon River once brought our newlyweds to the coastal resort of Vung Tau. On the way, the trees on the riverbanks had appeared so untropical, so alpine, that the bride was heard to exclaim, "Why, this is just like Switzerland!" For their honeymoon, our newlyweds were planning another trip to Vung Tau, "by way of Switzerland!"

The bride's knowledge of Switzerland was limited to watching one episode of an award winning Canadian-produced travel television show that comes on every Wednesday.

The yellow walls of Serenade are adorned with ornately framed paintings copied from postcards bought at the Louvre. There is a Watteau, a Boucher, and several Renoir nudes. Their feathery flesh is rendered even tremblier through the hazards of painting from bad reproductions.

Several witnesses swore our newlyweds had a sustained and shrieking argument just before the unspeakable happened. One or two reported they were tussling and yanking each other's hair. Still others claimed they were merely kissing and groping in a drunken display of public sex.

They had shared a sagging bed in a mini-hotel room without air conditioning two years before their church wedding. It was her first time and she had her right forearm lying across her face, concealing her tightly shut eyes.

A shoeshine boy was squatting on the opposite sidewalk when he saw, he claimed, the groom fall first, "like a large crow," followed by the bride, "fluttering like a butterfly." A one-legged beggar claimed they fell together, "intertwined like a soccer ball or a ball of thread."

They nearly landed on an aging American couple making their first visit to the Far East. A spring roll the husband had eaten that morning was rearranging most of his internal organs. His wife was having the time of her life. "I've seen a million things I never would have seen!" she kept chirping.

Considering the weight (him, 148 pounds; her, 120 pounds), shape, and mass of the falling bodies, resistance and quality of air (dusty, humid), it is estimated that, falling separately, the groom hit the ground in 1.2 seconds, and the bride, with her dress serving as sort of a parachute, in 1.5 seconds.

If they had been holding hands or falling on the moon, they would have hit the ground at the same time.

He was thirty-two and she was twenty-seven. "I don't want to have any children," she had said. "Wait until you're thirty," he replied knowingly. "Never," she said.

Pain is always private. Even when two people are experiencing pain at the same time, they cannot empathize with each other.

"Why were you looking up at that moment?" a reporter asked the one-legged beggar.

"I was lying on my back on the sidewalk."

"And why were you looking up?" the reporter asked the shoeshine boy.

"I heard a scream."

Scribe to beggar: "Did you hear a scream?"

"No."

It is said that most people who jump off the Golden Gate Bridge do so looking towards San Francisco instead of the Pacific. Rushing towards death, one must insist on a fine view. We must assume, likewise, that as our newlyweds leapt off the roof of the Majestic Hotel, they were not looking towards the Saigon River but down the length of the most elegant street of their home city. Once more, they could glimpse, if only briefly, the Paloma Café, Givral, Brodard, the old opera house, and far off in the distance, the twin towers of Notre Dame Cathedral, where only two hours earlier they had sworn to give each other all the remaining hours of their lives.

A man returned to the city where he had lost his virginity. After days of searching, he discovered it beneath a park bench, in the shape of a pebble. When he placed it in his mouth, he thought that it tasted pleasant, not unlike vanilla.

An old woman fell asleep plucking an old rooster. When she was awakened by the sound of cockcrow the next morning, she went outside and saw a headless and featherless rooster crowing.

The day before he was to go to war, an adolescent boy wrote a long letter to a girl he barely knew to suggest that they go skinny dipping in the lake "one of these days."

A grim-faced student walked into a mammoth bookstore and asked for a collection of poems by an unknown poet in an unheard of language. When the smiling manager suggested he try another bookstore, the student stabbed the manager with a fountain pen, killing him instantly.

A widower saw his dead wife in a supermarket and decided to follow her around. She was buying all the things they had never eaten together: olive oil, pate, imported pasta sauce . . . "She has a new lover," he concluded.

Hearing a timid knock late at night, a woman opened her apartment door and saw a hideous-looking man she did not recognize. After she let him in, he explained to her that they had met at a party twenty years earlier. They had kissed, and although it was a very brief kiss, the experience had haunted him until that day. "We did more than kiss," she corrected him, "I think you raped me." "No! No! No! No!" he said, "that was at a different party."

Planning on robbing a taxi at gunpoint, a man gave the driver an address in an out-of-the-way neighborhood. On the way there, they had to take numerous detours because of traffic jams. After several hours, they still had not reached their destination. Embarrassed, the driver suggested that they stop by his mother's house for a home-cooked meal, then continue afterwards. After a few glasses of wine, the man confessed to the driver that although he had planned on killing him earlier in the evening, he was now "very much undecided."

After becoming pregnant, she developed an intense hatred of the color red. She threw away all her red dresses and all her red underwear. She destroyed all the roses in her garden. She started to wear black lipstick. She would not leave the house at dusk, for fear of looking at the red sun.

Before he breathed his last, they led him outside to look at the sun for the last, and first, time.

~~~

Travel books fascinated him so much that he spent his entire life chained to his desk, with the curtains drawn, reading them.

~~~

He loves maps for their own sake, it is true, and when he shouts out while pointing at a random destination, "I want to be there," he is not expressing a desire to be anywhere, particularly, on this great earth, but only a wish to be a fiber, a speck at most, on an intricately folded, colorful piece of paper.

~~~

After half a century, a man returned to the city of his birth to discover it practically unchanged: all the old buildings were miraculously intact, although yellowing slightly, and the entire population of half a century ago, 2,489,863 souls, by exact count, were still alive, although yellowing slightly.

~~~

Two men were life-long enemies because of a word said decades earlier, a word misheard, misinterpreted, and exceedingly trivial, in any case, to any objective observer, a slight inflection, some say, a thread of air escaped from between more-or-less-closed lips, or a twitch of the eyebrow, and yet the results were the horrifying death of one man, and the maiming of the other.

～

He ignored public fascinations with movie stars, athletes, states-men, revolutionaries, mass-murderers, and poets by writing well-researched, footnoted, and illustrated biographies of bus drivers, cashiers, beauticians, filing clerks, plumbers, and roofers.

～

At the border between there and there, a young man who was caught with a generic secret inside one of his bodily orifices was forced to swallow a strong doze of laxative, then whisked to an insane asylum, where he spent the remaining years of his productive life.

～

Slang is crowding out real words, he foolishly thinks, forgetting that every word belongs to the shadowy vocabulary of an illicit crowd, invented to reassure and flatter its speaker, and confuse outsiders to what is being said.

～

The pretty woman confided, "Whenever I closed my eyes I would see its aerodynamic head, its black turf, its angle, and then suddenly the phone would ring, dispelling my vision."

〜

After his fifth gin and tonic, the scrawny, asthmatic man known as Uncle Moe divulged to an empty ashtray, "Yes, I must have known more than a thousand of them, but I've never known any of them more than twice."

〜

There, he could appraise them without the anxiety of actual contact, without stripping himself, a pseudo yes to a usually no situation.

〜

On an unseasonably cold night near the corner of Broad and Pine, one dandy said to another, "Yes, yes, life is short, and we are the beneficiaries."

〜

Resigned, the single woman begins each conversation with a male stranger: "We're only talking because you want to fuck me."

〜

He has traveled around the globe a thousand times just to spill his seed on the carpeted floors of unheated hotel rooms.

~~~

At forty, the bachelor decided to travel, to see the world, and among the many marvels he discovered, he was dismayed to find out that women everywhere, judging from the evidences gathered through the thin walls of hotel rooms from Brussels to Johannesburg to Riga, always vocalize their pleasure during sex, and that men, any man, really, always last minutes and minutes longer than him, which explains, finally, why he was still a bachelor after so many years, despite the good looks and charms that had attracted countless women to him *initially*.

~~~

The well-matched couple remain childless after five years of marriage, and now sleep on bunk beds, him on top, her on the bottom, although they flip-flop occasionally.

~~~

Suddenly she couldn't remember her husband's birthday, her children's names, his face, whether she had ever cheated on him, whether she was even married.

~~~

A boy was born on the luggage carousel at Singapore's Changi Airport, spent his infancy in the storage room of the baggage claim, grew into a happy, healthy child prancing around the beautiful atrium of the food court (often serenaded by classical music), had regrettably brief friendships with people of many nationalities, had sex for the first time, with a backpacker of indeterminate ethnicity, behind the check-in counter of the Royal Brunei Airlines (terminal 2), read the biography of Lee Kuan Yew and many bestsellers, spent much of middle age brooding in the departure lounge, then died, of abdominal hernia, in a well-scrubbed stall of the men's room.

Convinced that war is the only authentic game, the only game worth playing, he dedicated himself to being a mercenary, and proceeded to participate in the Pakistani-Indian War of 1971 (where he lost a finger), the Yom Kippur War (where he lost his right foot), the Falklands War (where he lost the right side of his face), the Gulf War (where he lost the left side of his face), and the 1995 civil war in Sierra Leone (where he lost another finger).

~

A fake life is not redeemed by a real death, he finally realized, as orange flames licked his angry eyebrows.

~

Before becoming a national icon in his youth, he languished for decades in cold, inhospitable countries, loveless and lampless, working an assortment of bullshit jobs that deeply offended his sense of personal greatness, his destiny, which he came to understand as the punishment of the people he had left behind, the wreaking of havoc on his homeland, when he would return.

~

He is a lifelong ingrate, having betrayed everyone—lovers, friends, relatives, dogs—who has ever benefited him, on principle, but he is strangely loyal to one whom he has never met, who has done nothing for him, who does not even know that he exists.

⁓

To your less-than-delicate question, Sir, I can only respond: Of course I would do it all over again, because even though I've lost my left eye, and my right ear, and my nose, and both of my legs, I've experienced something truly different, truly amazing, and have managed to escape an absolutely meaningless life that was slowly killing me back home.

It is true that a man carrying a book is always accorded a certain amount of respect, if not outright awe, in any society, whether primitive or advanced. Knowing this fact, Pierre Bui, an illiterate bicycle repairman from the village of Phat Dat, deep in the Mekong Delta, took to carrying a book with him wherever he went.

Its magic became manifest instantaneously: beggars and prostitutes were now very reluctant to accost him, muggers did not dare to mug him, and children always kept quiet in his presence.

Pierre Bui only carried one book at first, but then he realized that with more books, he would make an even better impression. Thus he started to walk around with at least three books at a time. On feast days, when there were large crowds on the streets, Pierre Bui would walk around with a dozen books.

It didn't matter what kinds of books they were—*How to Win Friends and Influence People*, *Our Bodies, Ourselves*, *Under a Tuscan Sky*, etc.—as long as they were books. Pierre Bui did seem particularly fond of extremely thick books with tiny prints, however. Perhaps he thought they were more scholarly? In his rapidly growing library one could find many tomes on accounting and white pages of all of the world's greatest cities.

The cost of acquiring so many books was not easy on Pierre Bui's tiny bicycle repairman's salary. He had to cut out all of his other expenses except for food. There were many days when he ate nothing but bread and sugar. In spite of this Pierre Bui never sold any of his precious volumes. The respect accorded him by all the other villagers more than compensated for the fact that his stomach was always growling.

Pierre Bui's absolute faith in books was rewarded in 1972 when, during one of the fiercest battles of the war, all the houses of his village were incinerated except for his leaning grass hut, where Pierre Bui squatted trembling but essentially unscathed, surrounded by at least ten thousand books.

# Viet Cong University

When I tell people I went to VCU, they usually ask, "Viet Cong University?"

"No, Virginia Commonwealth."

Talking of Viet Cong Universities: when a squadron of Viet Cong took over the ARVN officers' club at Tan Son Nhat Airport on April 30, 1975, they opened a fridge and saw twenty cans of Coke. Noticing a tab on each can, their officer, a man whose face resembled a backhanded fist, explained: "Hand grenades. A special kind. That's why they're being kept in this cold box."

The Viet Cong took one of the grenades outside and flung it against a burnt out jeep. It clanked off the side but did not explode. A black, fizzing liquid oozed out.

"Chemical weapon," the officer explained, "like Agent Orange."

A mangy dog came by to lap up the black, fizzing liquid. He was still seen to be alive a week later.

# Elvis Phong Is Dead!

I remember April 30, 1975, very well. I was sitting in my office at *Viet Rock!*, overlooking Nguyen Hue Boulevard. I could hear distant explosions and nearby gunshots. No sirens, strangely enough. Get away from the window, I thought absentmindedly but did nothing. I felt fatalistic that day, and wanted to be *implicated* in history, a vain and pompous notion. In any case, I had my radio turned on to the American station, in an early bid for nostalgia perhaps. Someone was singing "I'm Dreaming of a White Christmas." Sick, absolutely sick!, the American sense of humor. A few blocks away, people were clawing at each other and trampling on bodies to get aboard the last ships to leave Saigon. I should have been among them. Communist tanks were rumbling in and I was going to be toast as the foremost rock and roll critic of Vietnam.

As I stared down on the anarchy at street level my phone rang. A hysterical voice screamed into my right ear: "Elvis Phong committed suicide!" The chick hung up before I had a chance to ask questions. I grieved for a brief moment—Elvis was a good friend of mine—before I started to chuckle. A brilliant gesture, I thought. On the day the music died Elvis also had to die.

For the sake of foreigners and the ignorant, I will have to state the obvious: Elvis Phong is the greatest figure in the history of Vietnamese rock and roll. He created a revolution in Vietnam. Even his clothes were original. He often wore open shirts to show off his smooth, hairless chest, and rhinestone studded, fringed jackets even in 100-degree heat. An entire generation imitated Elvis Phong. He defined his generation. Elvis was Vietnam.

Ah my generation, those years! So much happened and so much has been forgotten already: American and Korean soldiers strutting on the streets, jets and helicopters, good whisky enjoyed from a bar stool, miniskirts and high hair, Elizabeth Taylor and Bruce Lee on the big screens, *Planet of the Apes*, random shellings in the provinces, propaganda banners strung between tamarind trees, cross-dressing draft dodgers, corpses with beatific faces staring at you from smudgy newspapers, the weight of a hand grenade in your callous hand, introduction of pizzas to the elite . . .

From the very beginning, Elvis was in sync with his time. His career coincided with and mirrored the Vietnam War. The Vietnam War made the man, made him write music, made him sing. In an interview published in *Viet Rock!*, June 22, 1967, Elvis Phong famously declared: "The din of hate provides the backbeat to my love songs." During live concerts, Elvis would shout to his screaming audience: "I write broken songs for all you broken people!"

Broken they may be, but there's no denying their tremendous power. Elvis penned over one hundred hits in his career. He emerged in 1963, the year Buddhist monks were burning themselves and President Diem was assassinated, with "Nhip Mua" ["The Rhythm of the Rain"] and "Thoi Vao Gio" ["Blowing in the Wind"].

In 1965, as U.S. Marines were landing on the beach in Da Nang, Elvis wrote "Vua Xa Lo" ["King of the Road"] and "Bat Duoc Cung Roi!" ["I Got You Babe!"].

In 1967, as the Cu Chi tunnels were being discovered, Elvis released "Chao Ong, Chao Ong" ["Good Morning, Good Morning"], "Mot Ngay Trong Cuoc Doi" ["A Day in the Life"], and "Tret Cai Lo" ["Fixing a Hole"].

In 1968, the year of the infernal Tet Offensive, in which 64,000 people were killed, 120,000 injured, 630,000 left homeless, Elvis released what must be considered his magnum opus, a monster compilation of delirious songs called *Dia Trang* [*The White Album*]. White, one must remember, is the Vietnamese color of mourning.

Among the many hits from this great album: "Cuong Dien" ["Helter Skelter"], "Tro Lai Nga" ["Back in the USSR"], "Toi Qua Met" ["I'm So Tired"], "Trong Khi Ghi Ta Cua Toi Khe Khe Khoc" ["While My Guitar Gently Weeps"], "Ob-La-Di, Ob-La-Da" ["Ob-La-Di, Ob-La-Da"], and "Hanh Phuc La Mot Cay Sung Am" ["Happiness Is a Warm Gun"].

# A Plane Ride

My wife sobs, "How will we know which plane to get on?" She looks so old when she's worried. "They'll show us at the airport, dear." I am not sure myself. We have been on boats, many boats, but never on an airplane. We have also been on cross-country buses.

My wife is packing grapefruits, bananas, yogurt, hard-boiled eggs, and fried chicken into a plastic bag. A bottle of aspirins also, two bottles of spring water.

"It's only a one-hour flight," I remind her.

"You actually believe what they tell you? When we get on a bus, they say it will take a day, maybe two, but it always ends up taking weeks, if not months!"

It seems like only yesterday we were pushing carts up a hill. And the day before that, crawling on all fours. O the rapid advances in modes of locomotion!

Approaching the airport we are elated with anticipation, a novel sensation. Prior to today, the airport did not symbolize for us release or adventures, but only the cruelties of life's essential promises. It was like a magnificent gate bolted shut permanently, erected only to humiliate us, with banquet noises, like rumors, faintly echoing from the other side.

But today is different. Today we will be departing. We are actually going up to the sky and soon we will be out of here. Soon we will be departed. The word "departure" rings euphonically in our ears. The word "arrival," on the other hand, strikes us as uniquely horrific; we are so focused on departing that we have forgotten we will be arriving somewhere else. Destination is not at all important, only departure.

We enter the airport's magical confines without a major incidence. And they really do show us which plane to get on. But first, they must frisk us for daggers and books. They must also sniff our shoes and try to dislodge the fillings from our teeth. They take turns peering into our crevices. It's a miracle they don't just strip us naked before they allow us onto the plane. We would happily consent to it, in any case. They liberate us from our wallets, of course. A man grabs my stiff, shiny ticket and pretends to tear it to pieces. Our gathering relatives sob and pass out.

As soon as we are allowed, we run down the runway and jostle the others up the stairs. I clutch my wife's hand. She screams. Someone punches me in the face. I step on a tiny body then lose both of my shoes. There is so much violence but it will all be worth it.

We have never seen the inside of an airplane before. This plane's compartment is as big as an ark or a whale. My sense of wonder is compromised, however, by the sights of my fellow passengers. Most are slovenly dressed in clownish outfits, tailored just yesterday specifically for this trip: tuxedo jackets over floral pajamas, T-shirts and skirts worn backward . . . I hope my wife and I do not look nearly as preposterous. Not all of us deserve such a fine fate, certainly, and yet here we all are.

Walking on thin carpet, surrounded by cushy seats, our lives are already transformed. We feel deeply embarrassed yet profoundly hopeful. This luxury must prefigure more luxury to come. Such hard plastic, such soft lights, such vinyl. We wouldn't mind being confined to this beautiful vessel for the rest of our natural lives. We feel absolutely safe inside here. Inviolable. Even if the plane should explode in midair or dive into the ocean, we would still have achieved our primary objective. We still have our doubts, of course. How can something this big get off the ground?

But before we know it, we are strapped to our new destinies. The man in front of me tilts his seat back and rests his head on my lap. I resist the natural urge to caress his wrinkled forehead, so much like my father's. Such a lapse into intimacy would have dire consequences, I remind myself. The man wears a shiny suit and looks like a government official. Surely enough, when I open a newspaper I see him on the front page, cutting a ribbon. Both in print and in life, he grins at me menacingly. My wife is oblivious to this renewed threat. Giddy for the first time in so many years, giggling, she peels a banana.

A lady in a brown uniform is telling us what to do should the plane crash. "Your shoes will sink but your hats will float," she informs us. "But don't you embarrass us," she suddenly growls, deepening her shrieking voice, "after you get off this plane."

My wife peels her second banana. I eat a chicken wing, then some yogurt, then a hard-boiled egg. Then I take a quick swig from a tiny bottle of whiskey bought at the airport gift shop. Suddenly the plane roars down the runway. My wife covers her ears and screams. The plane tilts upward. It lifts! I can't believe it! We're out! We're actually out! With a tremendous heave, I slop vomit all over the upside down head resting on my lap.

From the sky, our city looks very beautiful. On the ground it is a cesspool.

The sun shines on the silvery river. The houses are so tiny. The people are so tiny. Their pain must be so tiny.

All wars and diseases are below. All the unfortunates are below. We are above the clouds, finally. This earth is really round. That fact alone is making everyone ecstatic. We are finally at peace now. Many people are clapping, some are weeping openly. I give my wife a big hug. We kiss for the first time in maybe twenty-five years.

In the year 2049, a floating community was discovered eighty miles off the coast of Guam. On eleven rotting boats, lashed together by ropes, were ninety-nine individuals of indeterminate nationality. The last of the Vietnamese boat people? Descendants of lost Japanese soldiers from wwii? Australian naturists? With a single rusty nail, they had scratched hieroglyphic narratives onto the surfaces of their boats. It was determined that they had survived on flying fish and rain water. Most of them had never seen land. (The ones who had seen land were considered schizophrenic by the others; the hieroglyphs for "land" and "schizophrenic" were the same.) The sea, as the final resting place of their ancestors, was revered as holy and toxic. God dwelled in the lowest depths and was referred to as "The Biggest Lamprey." Their creation myth begins: "In the beginning, this monotonous earth did not bobble . . ."

It is often said that grammar provides a sure index to human behavior. Who hasn't noticed that people who write in run-on sentences are also prone to lying, to getting up late, and to alcohol? And those who do not punctuate at all tend to wear oversized clothes?

In an effort to inject more pep and resolve into its lethargic citizens, the government is mandating the use of an exclamation mark at the end of each sentence, spoken or written. "It looks like rain!" for example, or "I must sleep!"

It is now also unlawful to omit an exclamation mark from the end of key words. Key words are so numerous, however, that many citizens have found it safest to exclamate each syllable. "I! Am! A! Day! La! Bor! Er!" for example, or "Is! This! The! Ex! It?!"

Yesterday, an elderly gentleman who forgot to exclamate "frontal" in a private conversation with his wife (overheard by a vigilant neighbor) was sentenced to thirty-five years of hard labor to set an edifying example for the next generation.

You are often hunched over in an armchair to confide sweet nothings
to the side of a face. In this sense, you resemble a bassoon. Though you
expect the most extravagant praises for the most trivial accomplish-
ments, you shun and despise those who view you favorably.

As sunlight slants down on another late afternoon, you are strum-
ming on a guitar, eating shepherd's pie, and sipping rum-laced coffee.
Always bitterly exuberant, you see life as a pink spathe swathing a
yellow spadix. Tonight, standing in a musty hallway, you will speak
your penultimate line with some dignity.

You are often seen in profile at the top of a stairs, listening to a distant
music. Your hair is bouffant in the front, flat in the back. Your best
view is three-quarter. A minute or two after midnight, champagne
will spill from your fragrant mouth.

As you bend down to retrieve a long lost favor, someone seizes you
by the shoulder. You are such a master at aestheticizing your crimes
that even your victims are grateful to be included in the horrible
photographs.

Inducing doubt and self-hatred in all those you come into contact
with, you are a cancer and a pig. When a stream of your indulgent

LINH
DINH

reveries is nixed by an unpleasant, ghastly image, you let out a high C and touch yourself immodestly.

"A straight line is easy enough," you hear in a dream, "but it is not possible to draw a perfect circle." You smirk at this provocation. Waking up, you work all night on an endless piece of paper, drawing circle after circle, each one wobbly, obloid, squarish, rectangular, some are outright triangles.

Trying to peel away your fingers, someone pleads, "Let go of me!" but you are already beyond discretion. Like every other human being, you crave a single moment of absolute exposure. Today will be your day. Your veins will pop out.

Overhearing "Where I come from, people don't . . ." you punch the speaker, a blind, elderly immigrant, in the face, knocking two teeth out, before you yourself are knocked unconscious by a blunt instrument from behind. Waking up days later, you are told by a lugubrious dog that he, too, has often slept through the best parts.

In the men's room of a small town bus terminal, you discover your oil portrait in a trash can. You cut the canvas out, then stuff your folded face into your back pocket. Later, you notice with irritation that where your nose should be is a clay pipe, and your mouth is just a hole.

You cannot understand the story of a youth who falls in love with his own reflection in a spring. Where you are, water does not reflect.

Nothing reflects. One's view of oneself is made up entirely of other people's verbal slanders.

Told by your employer to buy a new shirt, you respond, "To buy a new shirt is to assume that I have at least two more years to live. Such presumptuousness cannot go unpunished. What's more, there would be this outlandish incongruity between a brand new shirt and my already worn-out body. Such an incongruity would cause my entire being, every single cell, to feel an unspeakable shame, a shame not on the skin, but in the skin, a shame to bring on my early death."

You wake up to a jungly tune. On the ceiling is a water stain showing your mother's face in three-quarter view. A suspicious fluid drips on your forehead. You wish there were a hand the size of an umbrella to protect you from all this fresh degradation.

65

13

In China, they bury eggs for a thousand years so their offspring can enjoy them later. In India, holy men dine on the cremated remains of angels. In America, buffaloes have wings and the cowboys gnaw on them between chaws of tobacco. They also snack on oysters that tumble down the Rocky Mountains.

I have a friend who lives on the twelfth floor of a filthy high-rise. The elevator has been broken for years and so, several times a day, she has to trudge up and down a dank, dark stairway reeking of human spillage. Her tiny apartment, though, is monastery clean. Its walls are lined with shelves of cookbooks in several languages.

Much of this woman's ridiculously small salary, from working in a shoe factory, is spent on these books. She loves to brood over the fantastic dishes described in them. Their ingredients are often so exotic, so bizarre-sounding, she can only imagine what the words are referring to, what they must taste like. (These cookbooks are so cheap they have no photographs or illustrations.) What is basil exactly? Or parsley? Pone? Pimento? Cumin?

Each word offers a different taste. Some have volume but no density. Some emit crude, rustic sensations. The most intriguing leave paradoxical, even tragic, consequences on the tongue.

By calling an old dish a new name, my friend believes (or allows herself to believe), you're already changing its taste. One does not eat bread but baguettes. One does not eat instant noodles but pasta. A beautiful girl with a hideous name becomes a hideous girl. An ugly girl with a pretty name becomes a pretty girl in print and in memory.

One can also *overlay* a dreary dish by conjuring up an exotic one. Each night, as she is slurping her usual dinner, Ramen Pride, you will find her hunched over the recipe for stracci integrali, Umbrian buckwheat noodles smothered in truffle oil and chicken livers. Or Odessa stew, tender beef cubes simmered in a dark sauce sweetened with prune skins. Or pollo en mole, a Mexican dish of boneless chicken in a broth of chocolate, raisins, almonds, and nutmeg . . .

"Do you know cheese has been around for five thousand years?" She asked me once, her eyes sparkling, "and I have yet to try even one variety! Their very names excite me: Gorgonzolla, Bel Passea, Gjetost, Raclette, Sap Sago. If you say Sap Sago over and over, Sap Sago! Sap Sago! Sap Sago! you have already tasted Sap Sago, whatever that is. A foreign word, like a foreign dish, resists the tongue at first, but you must learn how to swallow it anyway. To acquire someone else's taste is a moral act. A bigot loves his mom's cooking and nothing else. Do you know a wheel of Parmigiano weighs as much as a man, and must be cut by a saw?"

When talking, my friend has a habit of suddenly lunging forward, like a thoroughbred exploding from the gate. It is as if she wants to leap out of her clothes. Her arms are also swimming constantly to keep her body from drowning. I told her I have only experienced one kind of cheese, Laughing Cow, and cannot imagine any other. One kind of cheese is enough for me, I thought.

My friend shot me a brief, snorting laugh. She then declared that the variety of foods available in the world is the clearest proof that a person's range of experiences is indeed infinite, and that there's always room for change. A strange dish will transform a person. If Uncle Ho had tried guacamole, for example, he wouldn't have turned out the way he was. Only a sick man pretends he has *never* eaten peaches.

"Sexual promiscuity will dull the senses," she continued, her eyes enlarged and darkened, "but the reverse is true of one's appetite for food!"

"But you're not eating new foods!" I shouted, "only reading about them!"

"So be it! Cookbooks are my travelogues. They point to a truly vast universe, unlike pornography, which rehashes the same-old-same-old from three or four angles. That's why each day I must swim in these verbal stews. I'm sick of all the old words. A foreign word hints at, makes us conjecture, new adventures!"

To illustrate her point, she brought her sweating face closer to mine and scatted: "Pomodorifarcitimugginiarrosto!"

I very much wanted to interject that the reality behind a strange word is often just ordinary, or even less than ordinary, but I did not dare to contradict her.

There are times I suspect my friend would never actually try an exotic food. She's infatuated with words, not with matters. Words are all she'll ever eat. She's like a lifelong virgin who'll spend each night thinking about what other people are doing, the close-ups, the different combinations, whereas the rest of us, who fuck all the time, never think about sex anymore. She is sadder than the prisoners who regale each other with drawn out descriptions of meals from their distant past. At least they have eaten something. My friend wants to renew her interest indefinitely by keeping the actual experience at bay.

"What's more," she continued, "when you sample a new dish you are cannibalizing an entire culture. When I suck in a single strand of spaghetti I'm swallowing forty generations of Italians."

My friend's last thought conjured up several suggestive sentences in my head. I stared at her thin, open lips. I've often wondered.

"Do you know what olives are?"

"You must think I'm a complete idiot," I chuckled. "Everyone knows the story of Noah's ark. There was a pigeon on it that ate olives."

"Exactly! But have you ever seen an actual olive?"

"No! But neither have you!"

"The big difference between us," she declared, "is that I care about olives although I have never seen them. It's important to me that there are olive trees shading distant countries, and that somewhere, someone is eating olives."

To her mind, cookbooks are superior to any other kind of literature. "You will learn more about the English," she announced, "by pondering the recipe for grilled kippers than by reading all the plays of Shakespeare."

When she lived in the U.S. she would fantasize about Vietnamese food: bun mam, bun thang, cha ca la vong. When she lived in Vietnam she would fantasize about Italian food: spaghetti carbonara, ristotto nero, polenta con porcini. When she lived in Italy she would fantasize about American food: meatloaf, Kentucky Fried Chicken, Taco Bell.

Some of the richest people do not know that they are rich. They feel deprived, impoverished, and curse whatever god they do not worship for subjecting them to such a miserable (material) existence. But I am really not rich. I am poor. That's why I will tell you this parable about money.

~

Once there were two friends who had known each other since childhood. One was poor, one was rich. The rich one was so rich, he could not count all his money. (There is a saying: "If you can count your money, you ain't got none.") The poor one was so poor, a bee could live in his stomach. Why didn't the rich one help out the poor one?

He couldn't for many reasons, all of them valid. One: if he had leveled the difference between them to any degree, he would feel less rich, less like himself. His entire existence was dependent on this contrast. The poor one also valued this dichotomy. Thanks to it, he could indulge in all the pleasures of poverty: righteousness, resentment, appreciation of life's basic amenities, chronic alcoholism, stunted creativity, madness . . .

To both, their friendship was proof that people of different classes could intermingle. Like new lovers, they often paraded each other in public. In the evening, people would see them in one another's company, sitting at an outdoor café, one dressed carelessly, almost slovenly (the rich one), the other one in his finest. When the bill came, they would jostle each other to snatch it from the waiter's hand, with the poor one picking up the tab more often than not.

⌇

Once there were two friends who had known each other since childhood. One was poor, one was rich. One day the poor one said to the rich one: "I need a small favor from you. Please lend me some money so I can go into business. I promise I will pay you back within a year."

The rich one smiled. He was silent for a moment, then he said: "We've been friends for years now, but you have never asked to borrow money from me. I've often wondered why, seeing that you are so miserable. I have no idea how you get by from day to day. Although your clothes are always reasonably clean, they are very badly cut. Your shoes and your teeth are horrible. If you had asked me for a small loan years ago, I would have gladly given it to you, but you were always so proud, so stubborn, so righteous. I know you think yourself morally superior to me, because of your poverty. You imagine that I sleep all day while you labor. You assume that I have a long list of secret vices. Your vices, which are more than obvious, you attribute to the *sturm und drang* of your circumstances."

⌇

Centuries ago, there were two friends who had known each other since childhood. One was poor, one was rich. The rich one wanted to help out his poor friend very much but he needed a pretext. This opportunity came, finally, when his friend got married.

The rich one gave the poor one a ridiculously large sum as a wedding gift. The poor one was almost too embarrassed to accept it. This
money will transform me, he thought, turn me into a new person, a
process that will entail further embarrassment. He could already see
his neighbors laughing at him. They would now see his friendship
with the rich one in a new light. They would accuse him of sycophancy,
and of having had a hidden agenda all along.

Seeing her husband agonizing over this matter, the poor one's wife
suggested that they could jettison their past altogether by moving to
a new city. In a new city, they *could have* been born rich.

(Neither husband nor wife realized that a man is not an onion, and
cannot just peel himself off and become a new citizen. He can never
shed, only accumulate. Each state of being stains and accrues. At best
he can smear a rich coat of paint on his old, poor skin.)

After thanking his friend for his generous gift, the poor one
explained to the rich one that he would have to move to the capital to
go into business: "There are more commercial opportunities there.
I must go there for my future. But I will come back to visit you all the
time. And you must come and stay with us as often as possible."

For the first mile of his journey away from his past, the poor one
felt nothing but embarrassment. For the second mile, nothing but
rage. For the third mile, relief and nostalgia. As they clopped their
way towards a rich future, wife and husband held hands and thought,
*Finally, we've found our right destiny.*

Months and years passed but the poor one never came back to his
village. The rich one often wondered what had happened to his friend.
Did he fail in his commercial venture and was too embarrassed to

show his face again? Did he not even make it to the city, having been robbed halfway?

The roads were very dangerous back then. Rich travelers were often pounced on by brigands, who would strip them of all their money, jewelry, and clothes, and leave them stark naked, bleeding, or even dead, by the side of the road.

In his musing, the rich one even reproached himself for not having given his friend a sufficient amount to succeed in business. Even in my one instance of generosity, he thought, I revealed myself to be a cheapskate! He remembered with shame how he had intended to give his friend twice that amount, but had changed his mind at the last moment.

*I have to make up for this. I will bring him more money.* With that resolution, the rich one set out for the capital. He was dressed not like a rich man but like a beggar, to attract no attention from the brigands. Under his tattered cloak, however, he carried several fortunes in coins and gold.

In the capital, the rich one approached a man at random to ask about Mr. X, from Y Village. To his astonishment, the man knew exactly who he was talking about. "Everyone knows him," the man said. "He's the richest man in the city. He lives on Z Street."

Elated that his friend was still alive and doing well, the rich one set out immediately for Z Street. There he found an astonishing mansion, several sizes larger than his own. It even dwarfed the King's palace. It had so many fantastic architectural details, and was so lit up, that it appeared to be hovering in the sky, and not of this earth.

The poor one was entertaining a passel of literary men, maybe a hundred poets and novelists, when his servant informed him that there was a beggar at the gate claiming to be an old friend of his from Y Village.

"I am not from Y Village," the poor one said, "but give him a bowl of broth anyway. Tell him not to bother me again. If he should come back tomorrow, you can beat him on the head!"

X knew exactly who the beggar was, of course. "What is the matter, X?" a poet asked him.

X looked down at the grinning, sad poet, a proud, abject fellow, a sycophant and an aristocrat of the servant class. A wise, benign smile slowly blossomed on X's face: "There is justice after all. I was once dirt poor but I am now preposterously rich. My friend, who was the most arrogant of men, is now humbled."

# A Happy Couple

They are a happy couple during the day: he sitting in front of his computer in his office, she cooking in the kitchen. They have a one-year-old baby. At night, however, she curses him in her sleep. You asshole, she shouts. You motherfucker! He is philosophical about these insults. It's the airing of her unconscious, he thinks, and goes on sleeping.

But he has his outbursts also. He reaches across the bed and slaps her across the face. He punches, kicks, and strangles her. She punches and kicks him back. All during sleep.

In the morning, they wake up bruised and bloodied. They sit down to their breakfast cereal, their toes often touching beneath the table. He reads the sports page, absorbed by the box scores. She chatters on about what she wants to do with her day. The baby speaks in babyish gibberish. They look at each other and smile.

My wife and I are aware that people who are mentally ill are always imagining ants crawling on their faces while they're trying to sleep. But we are not mentally ill; our nightly nightmare is real enough: each night, a dozen ants crawl on our faces while we're trying to sleep.

In darkness, semiconscious and cursing, we try to brush these ants onto the floor, or kill them by crushing them against our cheeks. The ants retaliate by biting us. By the time a lamp can be turned on, however, all of the ants are gone.

In the morning, my wife angrily rubs the many fresh marks on her pale skin, glares at me and says: "It is all your fault!" But I have my own bite marks to rub also, and can only scrutinize the ceiling or the floor, trying to figure out where all these ants come from.

# A Moral Decision

A man found himself in the familiar position of being in love with two women at the same time. He was married to one of them and made the moral decision to remain faithful to his wife. He also trained himself to never think about the second woman, in an erotic way or otherwise. Occasionally, however, when he was slightly drunk or overly tired, he would think that the ideal solution would be for his wife to die a quick, violent death, so that he could consummate his love for the second woman within the context of matrimony, without being immoral in any way.

He is a huge man who loves to occupy tiny spaces. He is happiest whenever he has a chance to lie in a tent or stand inside a phone booth. In expensive restaurants he will suddenly duck under the table and make himself perfectly still and compact behind the stiff tablecloth. If his wife is wearing a dress (or even a miniskirt) he could disappear inside it for the better part of a day.

That one year I lived in New York I had an efficiency apartment in Queens. My job was also in Queens and so for an entire year I never went into Manhattan. I can't really say I know much about New York but what I got to know I really hated. I hated living there, I tell you, and I will never want to go back to New York, not even for a second. I don't even want to fly over New York, not even for a second, ever again.

Anyway, the window of my efficiency was perpendicular to a window of another efficiency. Each evening, I could see my neighbor standing in his kitchen, under his yellow light, washing the dishes, and he could see me, standing in my kitchen, under my yellow light, washing the dishes. Our windows were so close together we could have held a conversation if only we stuck our heads out our respective windows, but we never did.

My neighbor was a nice guy, nothing wrong with him, but the reason we never had a conversation, not even in the hallway, was because he didn't speak any English.

To all my attempts at small talk he would say "Yes, yes," then quickly walk away.

If I saw him in the hallway and I said: "How's it going, buddy?" He would say "Yes, yes," then quickly walk away.

If I said: "You feel like a beer, man?" He would also say "Yes, yes," then quickly walk away.

The few times he actually said something to me in actual English it appeared as if he had rehearsed that one sentence in his head for maybe a week beforehand.

The man was definitely foreign alright, though I could never figure out which country he came from. Maybe he came from South of here. Or East of here. Or West of here. Or North of here. Or maybe he wasn't foreign—maybe he was born in New York—and just never got around to learning English. Maybe he was retarded, or a foreign prince, I really had no idea.

Actually he was trying very hard to learn English. That's why I still remember him.

His method of learning English, though, was a little unusual. I had no idea what he was doing at first. Each evening, after six or seven, after dinner, I would hear him shout, for example: "Murder or suicide?! Murder or suicide?!" Over and over again. I could see him sitting at his kitchen table, shouting it. Or he would shout: "What is the most dangerous destination on earth?" "What is the most dangerous destination on earth?" Over and over again.

Soon I realized what he was doing was reading stories from one of the New York tabloids. He had his method. The retarded man, or the foreign prince, was very methodical. The retarded foreign prince would start from the very beginning: "A tourist was stabbed to death late last night in Central Park."

Then he would pause to look up the new words in the dictionary. (Even now, I can still hear the frantic rustling of the pages.) Since he didn't know hardly any, he had to look up just about every word.

Then he would shout out each word to himself (and to me, lying in my bed about ten feet away, trying to sleep). He would shout: "A! A! A! A! A! A!"

Then: "Tourist! Tourist! Tourist! Tourist! Tourist!"

Then: "Was! Was! Was! Was! Was!"

Then: "Stabbed! Stabbed! Stabbed! Stabbed! Stabbed!"

Then: "To! To! To! To! To!"

Then: "Death! Death! Death! Death! Death!"

Etc.

To get his pronunciation down, to sound more natural, he would also repeat the entire sentence several times: "A TOURIST WAS STABBED TO DEATH LATE LAST NIGHT IN CENTRAL PARK!

"A TOURIST WAS STABBED TO DEATH LATE LAST NIGHT IN CENTRAL PARK!

"A TOURIST WAS STABBED TO DEATH LATE LAST NIGHT IN CENTRAL PARK!"

Then he would continue with the next sentence: "His mutilated body was discovered by a jogger early this morning."

The whole process would start all over again, shouted out sentence by sentence, word by word, until late into the night and occasionally even until dawn.

# Losers

For most of my career on this earth, I've been a drunken housepainter
without a ladder. How did I end up this way?

I suppose I hang out with losers because they make me feel less
like a loser. I have my problems, sure, but I'm not quite as pathetic
as this motherfucker or that motherfucker.

What is a loser exactly? A man without money? A man without
social skills? Someone who can't get laid?

Jack has a shoe obsession. He likes to *buy* leather shoes and curl
up with them under a blanket. Men's shoes, women's shoes, it doesn't
matter. I've seen more than a dozen pairs on his bed. "Why are you
so promiscuous?" I've asked him.

Jim has a large collection of plastic dinosaurs. He observes that
dinosaurs strut around as if they're wearing high heels, a fact that
turns him on.

Joe collects sordid facts to entertain his few friends. "Do you know
that some sadhus eat cremated corpses?" "Do you know that Jeffrey
Dahmer liked to make love to an open wound?"

Jerry keeps a list of every woman who has ever smiled at him.
Another list tallies the instances of women touching his hands.

Jeff is a tall, good-looking guy. Although he appears normal in every
way, he still does not have a woman or money. All of his problems stem
from the fact that he cannot pronounce any word beginning with
an "w." No "weather," "war," or "wine." No "whips" or "wherewithal."

Instead of saying, "Would you like some wine?" Jeff would say, "You need a bottle?"

With his language circumscribed, Jeff is content to be an observer of men and things. If he could draw, Jeff would be an artist. He is a photographer instead. "I have a unique sex drive," Jeff said. "I'm aroused by the sight of a yawning woman. Each night I dream of diving into an open mouth." On Jeff's walls are hundreds of Polaroids of women yawning.

Every day she sticks her head out the window at 7:00 PM to water the plants she keeps on the fire escape. She waters her plants with a kettle, a very nice touch. I live one floor above her. I can see the top of her head. Her hair is shiny and the color of chestnut.

Sometimes I think I might want to call out, "Hey there!" but I never do.

Sometimes I think she might look up and see me, but she never does.

Although I work in a flower shop, Flowers I Love, I am not gay. My boss is gay. All the customers think I am gay.

I know I am not gay because I often think of my neighbor as I watch TV. I think of her as I kneel on the floor. Although I'm not good at remembering dreams, I can recall seeing her many times in my sleep.

I can smell her in my sleep. She smells just like a baby, like baby powder. I'm not sure why I'd think that. I've never been anywhere close to her.

Maybe it's because she has these small hands, with tiny fingers. Her wrists are also tiny. I do not like big-boned women.

I'm not a drinker, so I really don't know where to go to meet people. I do not like to sit in bars. When I'm in a bar, I can suddenly become very angry.

The last time I was in a bar, an older woman in a blue business suit was sitting next to me. "I'm from Florida," she said, "I work in real estate." She then told me that she liked this city very much, and that Philadelphians, contrary to what she had heard before she came here, are very nice. She asked me if I had read *Good and Evil in the Garden of Eden*. She bought me many drinks and said, finally, at last call, "You're really a very nice man, you know that? A very nice man."

My best friend is my boss, I'm sorry to say, although I don't really like to socialize with him.

My neighbor's name is "M Adams." That's all it says on her mailbox. Melissa? Marilyn? Mary?

My name also begins with an M. So we have something in common. My name is Mitch.

My mother's name is Eve.

I looked up M Adams in the phone book. There it was. I almost didn't want to find out her phone number. I waited a few days before I called.

"Hello?" she said. "Hello? Hello?"

I held my breath. I just wanted to hear her voice. I hung up.

She had a thin, reedy voice, like a canary. Already she was disappointing me.

A month ago I saw M walking in the street with a man. He looked just like M and they weren't holding hands, so I had to assume he was M's brother. I went home and knelt on the floor.

But then I thought, many people do date people who look just like them.

When I kneel on the floor I often look out the window. I can see people walking the streets. I can see girls, mothers, and babies. I can hear them talk.

My boss asked me, "Do you have a girlfriend, Mitch?" I said, "No." My boss said, "A beautiful boy like you without a girlfriend?"

I thought of taking roses or tulips from Flowers I Love and leaving them outside her door. I haven't done it yet. It wouldn't cost me anything. We throw away flowers almost every night.

I can be original and leave a sunflower.

Once I did something a little unusual. I went down the fire escape and looked into M's apartment. She was sitting on a couch, watching TV. All I could see was the back of her head, her chestnut hair. She was watching a show I absolutely hate. That was my second disappointment.

I went back upstairs and knelt on the floor. The spot is matted with old splatters.

When I see M in the lobby I do not know her. Once she said hello to me but I pretended not to hear.

It was such a breezy hello, she didn't mean anything by it. There was neither tension nor anticipation. She didn't even know me and yet she said hello to me? Does she say hello to everyone?

I read in the *Post* about a man who drilled little holes on the floor to peek into his downstairs neighbor's apartment. He watched her for about three years before he was arrested and given probation.

I don't see how he could drill holes into her ceiling without leaving debris on her floor for her to notice. Unless, of course, she wanted holes in her ceiling. Perhaps she had willed these holes into appearing in her ceiling.

It would be the highest compliment to have holes in your ceiling. After I read that article I imagined that there were many holes in my ceiling.

Do you know that crazy people sometimes prick themselves with needles? A crazy person feels trapped within his own skin. It's what separates him from the rest of the world. That's why he must puncture his own skin to ventilate himself.

And that's why I look out the window when I kneel on the floor. Sometimes I turn on the radio.

Sometimes as I look down at my neighbor watering her plants, I feel an irresistible urge to spit on her. I'm not sure why. I really do love her.

Once I saw M caress a chrysanthemum the way you would stroke the head of a cat. Whenever my attraction for M would start to fade a little, I would think of this scene to rekindle my passion.

If she were to die suddenly, say, in a car accident, I would feel a terrible grief remembering how she used to stroke a chrysanthemum the way you would stroke the head of a cat.

It's always good to have a love interest in your life. I cannot let M go because I have invested all this energy in her already. If I were to turn on this person, I'd be betraying myself.

But like I said, I really do love her. She has a way of tilting her head like a kitten, which I love.

Would M be attracted to me if she knew me better? It all depends on how sensitive she is, but these are my qualities:

Although I am not all that physically attractive, I am considerate.

I have no inordinate ambition. I do not need to dominate anyone, man or woman.

I hate all sports. The idea of sports is to create unequivocal winners and losers. I like to swim in that gray water where no one wins or loses.

I don't hate my mother.

I focus my sexual energy only on one person at a time. I don't like pornography.

I hate glamorous people.

I am not promiscuous even in thoughts. As I knelt on the floor, I'd think only of M.

I genuinely like to read the female novelists. My favorite poet is Emily Dickinson.

I know how to listen. I know how to pay attention to a woman.

There is nothing on TV tonight and I don't feel like kneeling on the floor anymore. I open my window and climb down the fire escape. The sliver of moon is a big cartoon smile in the sky. Everything will be fine tonight.

The lights in M's apartment are on. Her TV is also on. I climb quickly through the open window.

You cannot think about something forever. You must have the balls to step over that threshold, finally. You must dignify your desire with an act. Or at least an attempt. My name is Mitch and her name is M. We're M & M, so this is destiny.

My life has no repercussions so far. I need consequences, finally. I need a pillow and a mirror. Everything will be fine tonight.

Her apartment is spotlessly clean. A woman's touch, they call it. There is a white T-shirt slung on the back of a chair. I shudder as I touch it. The bathroom door is slightly open. It smells very nice. Soap and shampoo and perfume. I hear sounds of splashing water. Suddenly she starts to sing. Some stupid Broadway tune. Did someone see me climb through the window? I don't think so. Not very likely. As I nudge the door open, I clear my throat. My voice deepens: "Melissa?"

**LOVERS BY CHANCE** (1990) 2 hr. 6 min. This comedy opens with two strangers waking up in the same bed, naked and embracing. They are in neither one's apartment. They have not been to a party or a pub the night before and they are not hungover. They are not even sure they had sex. For the rest of this film and the rest of their lives they try to justify this original intimacy. (R) ★★★★★

**3 AT 3 IN THE MORNING** (1981) 1 hr. 14 min. An immigrant breaks into a sprawling suburban home of a white couple. After a confusing bedroom scene, dimly lit and without background music, in which various body parts are fleetingly glimpsed to be tied up and tortured, the threesome go downstairs to eat bacon and eggs at three in the morning. The dialogues are strained and tedious yet perfectly believable, with many desperate come-ons, Freudian slips, psychotic threats, and lame jokes. Oddly enough, all three actors, and not just the immigrant character, speak with a foreign accent. The night is indeed a foreign country. (R) ★★ ½

**MY GENERATION** (1976) 3 hr. 12 min. Vivid scenes of celebratory rioting are juxtaposed with fuzzy flashbacks of sibling incest. Features an amazing soundtrack. (R) ★★★★★

**PLANET OF THE APES** (2004) 2 hr. 22 min. Apes are encouraged to wear blue jeans, given English lessons. Enraged, they blow up the Capitol building. This remake of the sci-fi classic packs a wallop for its sizzling scenes of urban warfare: house to house combat, everything burning, civilian corpses. In one spectacular sequence, ape fighters trapped inside the Jefferson Memorial are blown to smithereens by our brave soldiers. The final frames show the president announcing to a relieved public that "we have prevailed." (PG) ★★★★★

**BLOOD AND SOAP** (2001) 1 hr. 35 min. A mass-murderer goes to a massage parlor to assuage his guilt. Stomach-turning scenes of outrageous carnage are interspersed with idyllic shots of naked girls soaping the murderer's muscular body. Enraptured men and women are shown sniffing bars of soap. Academic experts are also enlisted to expound on the pros and cons of various types of soaps. (R) ★★★

**A LAUGHING MAN** (1965) 2 hr. 35 min. A major film bio of the minor Austrian artist Richard Gerstl. Gerstl is best known as the painting teacher of Arnold Schoenberg and as Schoenberg's wife's lover. At the age of twenty-five, he burned most of his paintings and committed suicide. (PG) ★★★★★

**THROUGH THE VENETIAN BLINDS** (1998) 1 hr. 54 min. A documentary of a peeping tom, shot entirely with a Camcorder. John spends his evenings prowling around the suburbs of Chicago, hoping for brief glimpses of people eating dinners, watching TV, or sitting in front of their computers. He is particularly thrilled by *anything* seen

through venetian blinds. John denies that there is a sexual aspect to
his obsession, considering himself merely "a naturalist," akin to a
bird watcher, or "someone who gathers random impressions," a phrase
he claims to have gotten from Dostoievski. He also evokes Edgar Degas
to dignify his ogling women sitting on toilets. From all this, one might
assume that John is just a lonely creep yearning for a tender hand job.
What a surprise, then, to be introduced to his gorgeous wife, Gloria,
during the last ten minutes of the film. (R) ★★★★

**THE BADDEST NEWS** (2003) 1 hr. 27 min. A black Green Beret has
a white buddy who is killed during Operation Enduring Freedom.
After the war, he looks up the white man's father in rural Maryland
but takes a wrong turn at an intersection. (PG) ★★★★

**A DAY AT THE BEACH** (2003) 3 hr. 17 min. This feature-length
conceptual film surveys dozens of the world's beaches, from Vernazza
to Coney Island to Hainan to Kota Kinabalu. There is no narration.
Minutes go by without any sounds but the crashing of the waves and
the faint screams of seagulls. We see countless bodies, of course,
beautiful and not so beautiful, in various states of undress. There
are also boats, jet skis, and the occasional oil tanker. We also see a
whale and a man drowning. But the most mesmerizing shots reveals
nothing but water and sky. Nothing else. Watching this unusual film,
we become convinced that the generic ocean is all we're really after.
And that the desire to wade naked into the sea is a constant in all of
us. (PG) ★★★★★

**THE POSTMAN ALWAYS RINGS TWICE** (1996) 1 hr. 10 min. This Chinese flick has nothing to do with the *noir* classic by James M. Cain or the two American movies of the same name. Instead, it features a genial mailman who always rings twice at the six hundred–plus houses in his daily round for nearly forty years before he retires. (PG) ★★★★

**TAKING OFF!** (1967) 2 hr. 18 min. A nudie slasher space musical that will appeal to the nostalgic chainsaw mass murderer in all of us. (R) ★★★★★

**THE DREAMWORK** (1988) 3 hr. 6 min. Based on the book *The Dream Diary* by Basil Snell, in which the author records four thousand of his dreams over a five-year period. This tedious flick features only highlights from the book. Among them: Snell ordering Chinese food in an Italian restaurant, Snell driving backward through Harlem, Snell making love to his doppelganger. While some of the dreams are amusing enough, Snell often forgets that most dreams are only interesting to the dreamer. Snell has said in an interview that his entire career is inspired by one line from Bunuel: "The Sergeant would now like to tell us his dream from last night." (R) ★

**BORN AGAIN KILLER** (2000) 1 hr. 29 min. Many criminals find God while in prison. Ray King is unique in claiming that his born again status led him to kill. This documentary delves into the mind of the infamous Pennsylvania mass-murderer/rapist. King is a willing and earnest talker. He believes that God is the world's greatest mass-murderer. "Think of all the diseases and natural disasters and freak accidents and stuff." "I'm a Christian, and that's why I kill." "People are so vain, that's why you have to inflict pain on them." "You have to hurt them so they can repent before you kill them." "When people are in excruciating pain, they lose their vanity, and it brings them closer to God." "I have willingly given up my soul to bring people closer to God. I'm really a martyr." Only once did King falter in his theology. When asked why he raped many of his victims, Ray King could only come up with, "I guess I have a strong sex drive." (R) ★★★★★

**THE CREW** (1992) 8 hr. 0 min. It is true that the world of work is never properly depicted in movies. People are often seen making love, torturing and killing each other, but never enduring the tedium of work. Further, the occupations that show up most often in the movies are the relatively exciting ones, such as prostitution, soldiering, and firefighting, but never the mind-numbing and unglamorous ones such as accounting or plumbing or collecting trash. If movies refuse to acknowledge the vast netherworld of work, which makes up the bulk of our dreary lives, then can they be said to reflect real life at all? *The Crew* sets out to rectify this situation by following a house-painting crew for an entire eight-hour workday. We are introduced to a contractor, Joe, and his five-man crew: Hank, Tony, Chuck, Jeff, and Susan. (Yes, there is a woman on this crew. As Joe explains, "She's good at doing windows." And Jeff is a Japanese-American. "He's good at doing floors.") We see them arriving in the morning, all groggy and hungover. We watch as they set up ladders and drop cloths. We observe Hank standing on a forty-foot ladder sanding cornices, Chuck scraping paint from a window, Tony priming a door, Jeff filling holes in a bedroom, and Susan calking a baseboard. We hear them passing the time with banter and racist, sexist, and homophobic jokes. But most of the time all we hear are inanities coming from a tinny radio. Bad songs and commercials and Rush Limbaugh railing against "pencil-necked geeks" and inciting us to go to war. At lunch, we join the crew as they chow down on cheese steaks and potato chips. We hear Chuck exclaim: "These potato chips are really good!" Then more of the same: scraping, sanding, priming, caulking, and cleaning brushes. Also more jokes and more talk radio. As this movie drags on, we keep checking our watch while trying not to fall asleep. Finally, after seven hours and thirty minutes of this endless film, it's clean-up time! and we find ourselves just as relieved as the rest of the crew. We learn that everyone except Susan is going to a strip bar, but we don't get to follow them there. That's another movie. (PG) ★★★ ½

**HOUSEPAINTERS** (1997) 8 hr. 0 min. A rip-off of *The Crew*, employing professional actors. Instead of the many dead spots of the original, we are now treated to meaningful flashbacks, a bloody fistfight, and several shower scenes. The female of the crew is now a top-heavy bombshell who could never make it up a ladder in real life. (R) ★

I don't mind that my cellmate is a woman. His daddies buy him chocolate bars and cigarettes, which he freely shares with me. I also don't mind that he's an intellectual. I'm one also. In fact, we might be the only two of our kind here. In this place, if you can name more than two state capitals and recite the alphabet once without flinching, then you're considered an intellectual. But we are truly intellectuals. We know how to reason. The only difference between us is that I'm an organic intellectual, whereas he's an inorganic intellectual.

By inorganic I mean his logic does not coincide with logic.

He told me he's been obsessed with the shape of the scissors his whole life: "I like the fact that some have blunt ends, and some have sharp ends. They can stab, cut, and open wide, like a mouth." With his fingers, he made cutting motions over his nose, smiling mischievously. He also told me he's ecstatic to be in here: "All my life I wanted to come to this place, although I did not know it. There are no mistakes, only choices. Each of us chooses his own destiny."

That is nonsense. I did not choose to come to this place. No one chooses to come to this place. What landed me here was an illness, something extraneous to my person. No man can tell me that I would rather be here and not on the outside. That's why he is an inorganic intellectual. He makes universal laws out of his own confusions. He also said: "Once a man accepts his destiny, even if it is a monstrous destiny, involving much pain and suffering, his own as well as others, then he will be finally be calm, and in ecstasy!"

This from a man who's serving life without parole! What he did was certainly monstrous, but no worse than what I did, no worse than what most of the others in here have done. I do not hold that against him. I also do not expect him to be contrite. What I object to is the fact that he sees his crime as a vehicle towards self-discovery. "For a person to become fully himself," he philosophized, "many others have to be destroyed. It is true of nations also."

If that is true then I am not interested in becoming fully myself. I'd rather be half a decent man than a whole evil man.

I'm in here because I deprived twelve persons of their longevity. I'm not proud of that. I'm also sorry I will have to spend the rest of my own longevity in this concrete and steel zoo with a bunch of fucked up losers. (I served four years in the army, but that does not hold a candle to this.)

Before my weekly injection of Depo-Provera, a miracle drug that calms and attenuates my priapic ramblings, I was half man, half monster, but now the monster sleeps quietly inside my bowels, and I can safely be considered human again.

I was so wound up, so easily provoked, so spread thin that, with any stimulant whatsoever—a lingerie ad, a cup of coffee, a donut—I would think, Blood! I used to think of my body as one long knife, and each day a long thrust forward in search of my next victim.

In the beginning I just killed blindly, like a madman, with no philosophy behind what I was doing, but after my sixth or seventh victim (Diana? Susan?) had been quieted, when I had suddenly become the only person left in the room, I realized what I was after. I was not so much interested in snuffing out a life as in creating a bond with my victims through humiliation. (What is intimacy but shared humiliation?) After that epiphany, I would say to each victim before I slit her throat: "Now that we know each other's secrets, now that we've humiliated each other, there is nothing left for us to do but to meet in the next life. I love you."

I would become so moved by this declaration of love that tears would well up in my eyes. I would kiss the cold teeth of my women.

There is a strange silence after a killing. It is as if the corpse is absorbing all the noise of the world into its decaying orbit. Right after you've killed, you feel as if you're the last person left on earth. A wonderful, peaceful feeling. They used to blindfold a dozen or more slaves and force them to box each other in a ring until only one was left standing.

After my tenth victim, I felt so ecstatic I thought God would call me up. I kept staring at my phone, certain that it would ring at any moment. I was sure God would congratulate me for participating in his joke. A woman colludes with God at the beginning of the joke by giving birth. A man at the end of it, by killing.

My eleventh victim had her eyes wide open. It unnerved me a little. In a poetry workshop, I learnt about Imagism and Surrealism. I wrote: "The eyes are the soul's windows. When the soul has vacated its abode, all eyes should be closed." (My teacher, Mr. Silliman, complimented me for rhyming "window" with "soul" with "abode" with "closed.") I take all the classes they offer in this place. It's important to not waste time and to broaden your horizons.

But the biggest factor in the recovery of my sanity has been my correspondence with a pen pal, Julie.

Julie lives in Australia. She is thirty-nine, divorced, and has breast cancer. In the past, when other people's misfortune was my primary source of happiness, the last fact would have made me ecstatic. Now I send her comforting words. I also inject her with regular doses of my own miseries, exaggerating them when needs require, so she will feel better by comparison. Such is my concern for her well-being that I save the most horrible anecdotes of prison life for when she's truly down. Such is my sensitivity.

I also take care to balance the horrible with the merely amusing. In only my third letter to her I told her how the guard must look under my balls and into my asshole before I'm allowed into the yard. It's good to make a woman laugh. One good laugh might send her cancer into remission. But I can see you cringing. You've noticed that I've lapsed into a self-congratulating mode. Us cons are often accused of being self-serving. Enough of that. I must take a deep breath and change the tenor of this monologue.

Julie allows me to peep into her ordinary life. I've never been ordinary with a woman before. She tells me what she had for breakfast, what books she's reading. She describes to me the blouse she's wearing as she writes me her letter.

This letter from Julie is odorless. Paper has no smell. Still, it has been touched by a woman, a real woman made up of flesh and blood. That's why I press the letter to my nose and sniff in ecstasy. This is the best smelling piece of paper in the world. I am not embarrassed to admit that I've also rubbed it on other parts of my person.

Some guys in here abuse their pen pal privilege by asking women to sit on Xerox machines and things like that, but I'm not like that. In fact, I haven't asked Julie for any photographs.

Julie has never asked me why I'm in here. "We all have a regrettable past," she wrote, "I have secrets also. Every person has a right to hold on to his secrets. If all our secrets were exposed, we would be ostracized forever from human society."

"If I had met you ten years ago," I wrote, "I would not be in here."

I will never be able to embrace Julie in this life. Only in the next life. And yet I'm glad she lives so far away from me that I can never do anything horrible to her. Not that I would want to. Julie will never be my thirteenth. It's important for a man, any man, to have at least one successful relationship with a woman in his life. So now I've done it.

Doctor Fang, our psychologist, told me I was afraid of women in the past because they forced me to be fawning, considerate, abject, hopeful, and brave, all those qualities I never had, and never cared to develop. He said, "All you guys are afraid of women. That's why you're in here!"

There is a part of me that still believes I will get out someday. Maybe an earthquake or a revolution will cause the prison gates to be flung open. Maybe an invasion of aliens from outer space. Maybe a meteor.

Sometimes, in that moment just before sleep, when you're neither conscious nor unconscious, I see myself walking down Pine Street in Philadelphia. But you can't be walking down this street, I'd think, you're in prison! In my half-dream, I'm aware that I'm lying on my bunk, under a thin, itchy blanket, and yet I can still see, very vividly, the Last Drop coffeehouse, and across the street from it, Dirty Frank's tavern. If I concentrate real hard, I can open Dirty Frank's door and just walk right in. I feel a terrible rage rising up in me, open my eyes, and see the bottom of my cellmate's bunk.

Once, in this state, I called my cellmate a horrible name which I regretted immediately. When he woke up I excused myself by telling him I'd just had a nightmare.

My cellmate was married for five years. Five wonderful years, he says. "We had sex twice a week, a major argument once a month, cookouts and a trip to the shore every summer." But he threw it all away because he was obsessed with the shape of scissors.

"All through my life, I've had an unbearable urge to stab women. It was only after I'd stabbed my wife in her sleep, without provocation and with a pair of scissors, that I realized I had an unconscious desire to be imprisoned. I wanted to be among men. I wanted to be stabbed in return as a fulfillment of my destiny."

More than a century after his death, Stewart Crenshaw still provokes endless debates. With a single sublime or hypocritical decision, Crenshaw forever affixed himself to American history. Like Billy the Kid, Tokyo Rose, Muhammad Ali, or Jeffrey Dahmer, Crenshaw is an American icon, but whereas the others had to become outlaws to insinuate themselves into our consciousness, Crenshaw was never a criminal. Although he enslaved himself, he was never imprisoned. What Crenshaw did only went against the most deeply held beliefs of his time, and maybe even of our own.

In Friarspoint, Mississippi, Stewart Crenshaw is a cottage industry. There, his name graces (and defaces) just about every large building. Gift stores sell Crenshaw T-shirts, key chains, whips, banjos, chains, and mugs. There is a Crenshaw Diner where you can order a daily special of cornmeal, half a pig's foot, and a glass of water ($3.95). Crenshaw's rather generic face is immortalized with a bronze bust behind the beautiful courthouse.

Every day, dozens of buses carry thousands of tourists (mostly from Mobile, Alabama and from Japan) to the Crenshaw Plantation. The majority will ignore the big manor house to crowd into the ramshackle hut at the very edge of the property. Within its dim, narrow confines, they can jostle each other to take fuzzy pictures of the blanket on which Crenshaw spent countless nights groaning in happiness after another insufferable day spent out in the field hacking sugarcanes in one-hundred-degree weather. They can examine his boots, hammer, felt hat, wooden spoon, nails, and sickle.

A small plaque on the wall encapsulates Crenshaw's biography for the ignorant and the forgetful:

Stewart Crenshaw was born in 1802 in Savannah, Georgia. His father owned an ironwork and young Crenshaw grew up amid luxuries and a dozen books. In 1828, both his parents died in a fire. Crenshaw sold the family business and moved to Friarspoint, where he bought three hundred acres of uncultivated land (the very ground you're standing on). On this property Crenshaw built what he thought was a Georgian house, a smoke house, a barn, a stable, and slave quarters. Situated on a small rise, the Big House is distinguished for its axes of symmetry, straight lines, and deceptive angles. The long gravel road that leads to the twelve steps that leads to the colonnaded porch is shaded by two rows of cypresses. Spanish mosses, magnolias, and rose bushes grace the surrounding gardens.

Crenshaw was no farmer but he knew enough to decide that the black soil on his land would be ideal for sugarcane. He went out and bought twenty slaves, men, women, and children, at just over $700 a head, all belonging to one extended family. Then he did something that would shock an entire nation. Crenshaw told his new slaves that the Big House, and everything in it, was theirs to keep. He would move to a hut on the fringe of his own property.

The patriarch of the slave family was a man named Ezekiel Moses. Moses could not understand Crenshaw's bizarre decision. He was certain that this man was playing a trick on him. As soon as they took over the Big House, all hell would break loose. Angry white men

would rush over from the town to tie them to individual stakes then
set them on fire.

Crenshaw reassured Moses: "I just paid $15,000 for you'all. Why
would I allow them to burn my property?"

Moses stared into Creshaw's grinning blue eyes: "But why are you
doing this?"

"Because I am your master. As a master, I can demand that you
become *my* master. I have the right to be your slave."

"To be a slave is not a right," Moses corrected him, smirking.

"But you're wrong, my friend. Being a slave is the only right a man
has."

Moses knew he was talking to a fool. He would have laughed in
this fool's face if he wasn't so angry at him for making a mockery of
his people's misery. Moses spat on the ground: "So how long is this
game gonna last?"

"It's not a game, my friend."

"Are you *my* slave at this moment?"

"Yes, I am."

"Then stop calling me *friend*."

Moses waited a night to move his family into the Big House. For
the first week, they confined themselves to a single room next to the
kitchen. The vast manor house was taken over room by room. It took
Moses's clan nearly half a year to possess the entire structure.

Standing on the front porch each morning, Moses could see
Crenshaw working by himself out in the field, a tiny figure half hidden in the canes. The pale man hardly knew what he was doing. One
of Moses's sons would run out periodically to show Crenshaw the

basics of sugarcane farming. After sunset, someone would bring him rice, beans, and chicken gizzards. Crenshaw supplemented his meager diet by growing spinach and cabbage on a thin patch. Even without an overseer, he would work from sunup to sundown every day but Sundays.

Word soon got out of Crenshaw's strange behavior. Every day there was a mob outside the front gate. They did not dare scale the fence because Crenshaw had warned them, very loudly, that anyone who did so would be shot on sight. (Moses had lent him a shotgun for the occasion.) Among the merely curious and the hostile were abolitionists who extolled Crenshaw as a saint. "He's doing penance for your sins!" they would shout over the hoots and jeers. Newspapers from all over the country, and even a few from Europe, sent hundreds of reporters, but Crenshaw would grant none of them an interview.

Moses was not so reticent, however. Initially frightened by the volatile mob just outside his front gate, he gradually became used to their angry and joyous presence. At first he would stand in the window of the master bedroom on the second floor, peeking at the rabble through a tiny crack in the curtains. Then he would banter with them while standing on his front porch. Finally Moses would sit on a large chair just inside the wrought iron fence to answer their questions.

"Is Crenshaw a fool, Mr. Moses?"

"He's very brave."

"He must be mad!"

"He's also a genius."

"Why would you say that?"

"Only a genius can create a new paradigm."

"Can you repeat that?"

"A new paradigm."

"How are you treating him?"

"Like a son."

"Is he getting enough to eat?"

"I wouldn't want to starve him."

"What does he do in his spare time?"

"He prays."

"What else does he do?"

"He sings and he writes"

"He writes?!"

"Yes, he writes."

"What does he write?"

"A slave narrative."

"By oil lamp?"

"By candlelight."

"You allow him to do that?"

"I have nothing to hide."

"Does he complain much?"

"He's always cheerful."

"But he can't be happy!"

"He is lonely."

"Does he need a wife?"

"No, other slaves."

"Why don't you buy him some?"

"He doesn't believe in miscegenation."

Although the novelty of a white man slaving for a black man never wore out completely, the crowd eventually thinned until there were usually no more than a dozen spectators a day. Some days there were none. Crenshaw and Moses were allowed to return to the tedium and solipsism of their respective lives. The years passed . . .

Can a slave actually think in years? Not very likely. A slave cannot even think in days. One cannot conceive of a future one has no part in planning.

As Crenshaw got up each morning, he would feel nothing but dread, bordering on nausea. Sometimes he would throw up the miserable food he had eaten the previous night. He really could not believe what was ahead of him. Through the entire morning, he could only think of the cornmeal awaiting him at lunch. At some point in the early afternoon, however, Crenshaw would snap into a sudden calmness. His guilt, anxieties, and self-pity would all be gone. His mind would be so limpid it could range over everything. For maybe half an hour Crenshaw could forget he was a slave. But the late afternoon brought with it an even more intense dread than the early morning.

As Crenshaw lay on his itchy blanket late at night, his past would return to him as an appalling fantasy. It was always swarming with phrases and body parts. Savannah would be remembered as a brightly lit street, then as a dim house, then as a tiny basement room. The twelve books he had read would be reduced to the word "book."

Once, Crenshaw thought he would just march into the house and shout, "Game's over." *I'll teach that damn Moses a lesson!* He didn't do this, however, not because he had given Moses his word but because it would ruin his self-portrait. It would cheapen this story.

Living in the Big House, walking on carpet among the mahogany furniture, Moses refused to feel smug or vindicated. Any radical change in one's circumstances normally brings with it an embarrassed disavowal of the past and the realization that here, finally, is the truth. But Moses's composure did not allow him to become giddy over a mere reversal of fortunes. Though his present already felt more real, more authentic, than his past, he wasn't sure which was more of a mistake. When he was a slave, Moses would think, wistfully and desperately, that even his life had to count as human experience. He even thought that any life could be taken to represent human experience as a whole. Now he knew, once and for all, that any man's life is totally arbitrary, and represents absolutely nothing.

Moses's enjoyment of his new life was also sharpened and soured by flashes of anger. He never forgot that he was still legally, and essentially, a slave.

Although Moses and Crenshaw lived within sight of each other, they never entered one another's house's and they never exchanged more than a few words. Whatever either one said sounded like mimicry to the other. They may have swapped lives, but they still could not enter each other's universes.

When Moses was still a (real) slave, he could take paths through the woods to meet clandestinely with other slaves from nearby plantations. Now he was trapped within his own home. His world had actually shrunk. If he walked out the gate he would be considered a runaway and hunted down like an animal. Neither free nor truly a slave, Crenshaw and Moses were bound to each other for life.

In rare, bitter moments, Moses would curse Crenshaw for denying him the moral high ground, and the dignity, of being a slave, while still enslaving him.

In *his* rare, bitter moments, Crenshaw would curse Moses for denying him the moral high ground, and the dignity, of being a slave, while still enslaving him.

A real slave or not, Crenshaw felt slave enough. His existence as a slave became so relentless, so familiar, so inevitable, that he gradually came to think of it as the natural condition of man. Being a slave became synonymous with life itself.

On an April afternoon in 1861, Crenshaw decided to take a nap after lunch. He had never shirked work like that before. His last glimpse of this earth was of a starling flitting across a cloudless sky. His last thought was, I deserve this. Moses would not discover Crenshaw's corpse lying on the ground until three or fours days later.

Moses went more conventionally. He died of a heart attack at dawn on January 31, 1865.

In spite of what Moses claimed, it is not at all clear if Crenshaw ever wrote a slave narrative. No authentic manuscript has been discovered. Within a year after Crenshaw's death, more than a dozen volumes were published, all purported to be his autobiography. The heftiest one leveled off at just under three thousand pages. The slimmest: a five-page pamphlet. Among the unlikely titles were *Uncle Tom's Cabin*, *Absalom! Absalom!*, *The Autobiography of Malcom X*, and *The Joy Luck Club*.

Moses stridently denounced all these absurd books as travesties of
his slave's tragic and magnificent life. As a real slave, however, he had
no legal claims over his fake slave's intellectual properties. At each
opportunity, he would brandish a ream of mud-smeared manuscripts
as the only authentic writings of Stewart Crenshaw. No one took him
seriously. It was obvious to all those who had a chance to glean through
their messy contents that Moses was the true author.

Our house has nothing and a shopping center has everything. That's why my wife feels much more at home at a shopping center. "A shopping center is my ideal home," she said. "When I stroll through the wide corridors of a shopping center I am surrounded by all the things you do not provide me with. One moment my arms are brushing against a dozen fluffy mink coats and the next an effeminate man is spraying French perfume on my tired wrists. And when I am absolutely worn out from walking all day I can rest for a moment on a genuine leather couch."

# Costa San Giorgio

There is a street in Firenze, a real street—Costa San Giorgio—that is built like a tunnel. Twisting and narrow, its width hemmed in by imposing brick walls topped with colorful shards of glass, Costa San Giorgio goes on forever without being interrupted once by another street. The thin sky provides the only relief from claustrophobia. Costa San Giorgio undulates up and down, crossing several hills, or maybe just one hill in a zigzag fashion. Or maybe it is circular, a beltway rimming Firenze, all of Italy, or the entire known and unknown universe. Or maybe it is a high-tech treadmill. In any case, once the hapless pedestrian has entered Costa San Giorgio, he has no choice but to march on to his eventual, laughable yet tragic demise. Along the way he will notice, if he is observant, the touching remains of his equally hapless predecessors: single shoes, fountain pens, toothpicks, tufts of hair, small bones, pages torn from a novel. He can always backtrack, of course, but that rarely results in a happy ending—too much ground has been covered, too much time wasted. To backtrack would also be tantamount to admitting the foolishness and futility of one's entire life, a life wasted walking down Costa San Giorgio. And so the pedestrian must march on, on a sidewalk too narrow and too slippery for even a cat to prance on. And when he's beaten down by thirst and hunger, shame prevents him from knocking on any of the stern doors fronting the rare houses. In any case, these houses, although still sturdy and elegant, show every sign of having been abandoned centuries ago.

# The Self-Portraitist of Signa

You know how it is: it is late afternoon and you suddenly find yourself in the dreadful town of Signa, standing in a bright café with a cold one in your hand? Well, I am leaning against the bar holding a Peroni, my fourth or fifth, and surrounding me are middle-aged men in rumpled suits downing shots of amaro. The potato chips and peanuts are actually free. A pensive ten-year-old girl pauses in front of the cash register, postponing for a few seconds the precious purchase of a bar of Emozioni. But my attention, for the last two hours or so, has been diverted from all these folks to a woman sitting alone at a table. Conventionally dressed but in a pair of men's shoes, sitting alone at a table, she is drawing a series of self portraits with a set of colored pencils. Multiplied by an infinity of angles, the human face is really a kaleidoscope, an infinity of faces, and it is truly a miracle we can recognize each other (or ourselves) at all. But this woman has committed to memory all the essentials of her own physiognomy, and can conjure up, time and again, her own basic likeness without resorting to a mirror. She draws grimly yet fanatically, with an angry concentration that erases everything from the world but a tragic nostalgia for her own face. The café is transformed into a private monastery cell, with the rest of us reduced to dim ghosts blurring the edges of her bright vision. Each portrait is made to look different from the others: one depicts her as she appeared just this morning, at sunrise, emerging from a dream-racked sleep; another depicts her in the throes of love, just last night or maybe more than a decade ago; another depicts her as an anonymous child of three; and yet another depicts her as a marmoreal corpse, lying in a garlanded and perfumed coffin, awaiting our final nods of respect.

# Luisa Loves Her Husband

Luisa loves her husband very much and would never think of betraying him. Occasionally, however, while standing in the shower, she allows herself to fantasize briefly about other men. But these men are not so much men but archetypes, designed to be fantasized the world over by more-or-less virtuous housewives such as Luisa. Surely there is no harm in imagining oneself being arrested by a leering cop on a deserted highway at midnight or fondled by a taciturn priest redolent of baby powder or raped repeatedly by a charging and leaping soccer player as long as one doesn't think about these things while making love to one's, by now, all-too-reliable husband?

One does not—cannot!—go to Parma without bringing back some parmigiano cheese, of course, and thus it was only natural that Massimo Epifani, a native of Otranto, came back from a week-long trip to Parma with an exceptional wheel of parmigiano, aged for three years and weighting no less than ninety pounds. He barged into his house cradling his beloved cheese like a huge baby and, in his excitement, even forgot to kiss his lovely wife, Claretta, who had been waiting anxiously in the living room for at least half an hour to greet him. Although it was not dinner time he insisted on sampling the cheese right away. This was when everything quickly went wrong. According to one version, it was the wife, miffed at not having been kissed at the door, who started to hack at the cheese with a butcher knife, thus provoking her husband into a murderous rage. According to another version, it was the husband who did the cutting. It was his slow, tender handling of the cheese, accompanied by many unctuous comments, such as "The cows are very different in Parma" and "You must not *hurt* such a beautiful cheese," that broke his lovely wife's heart and drove her into a jealous fit of retaliation. According to one neighbor, she was heard screaming at the top of her lung: "Go ahead and kiss that cheese, why don't you?!" Someone then shouted "No no no!" (Or maybe it was "Yes yes yes!") In any case, by the time the carabinieri arrived half an hour later, there were only two pale corpses embracing on the floor, one male, one female, cut up every which way imaginable, lying in a vast pool of blood and cheese.

# A Worshipper of Beauty

Among the many beauty pageants that grace the end of summer none is more compelling, to this worshipper of beauty, than the Sleeping Beauty Pageant in Forte di Marmi. Let the vulgar flock to the Miss Underage Frontal Nudity contest in nearby Viareggio, the last day of August will always find me, front and center, with my mouth wide open and my eyes unblinking, with my chin resting onstage, at the Sleeping Beauty.

This year's event was particularly satisfying. Seventy-two contestants were flown in for the three-hour extravaganza. I could not wait for the lights to dim and for the gurneys to be wheeled out.

There was no music, of course. The MC spoke in a whisper. The audience had to be warned repeatedly by the stern ushers never to applaud. And out, finally, came Miss Amalfi! She was lying prone under a pink cotton sheet, her black hair radiating from her white face, her breathing irregular. With her mouth trembling slightly, she appeared to be trapped in a nightmare, a sight that moved many of the judges as well as the whole audience.

Next came Miss Bari, lying supine with her face turned away. All we could see was hair. No neck even. The back of a woman's head is not this man's idea of a turn-on. A tactical mistake surely! Who is Miss Bari's manager?!

Then came Miss Barletta, a classic sleeping beauty, serene,

oblivious, your sister (or mine) from that mythical summer night a long time ago.

Miss Cosenza left some of us gasping! With her bloodless lips and bluish complexion, Miss Cosenza was perhaps in a coma!

Miss Gubbio, at fifteen the youngest of the night's sleeping beauties, was seen lying on her right side clutching a stuffed bear, a contrived prop that fooled no one.

Miss Grosetto, at thirty-seven the oldest, was also clutching a stuffed animal, a python, an attempt at humor more pathetic than touching.

Miss Padova was passed out after too many drinks and sprawled across her messy gurney.

Miss Pisa, naked, was tossing and turning.

Miss Trieste was visibly pregnant and dozing fitfully under a mound of colorful blankets. In spite of the heat, she was wearing a thick pair of socks.

The progression of so many sleeping beauties, all beautiful, all sleeping, left me woozy by the end of the long night. The sight of a beautiful woman sleeping I will always cherish above all else in the world. Three times I had to reach out and touch the wheel of a rolling gurney. Is she sleeping yet? Of course she is sleeping! If only I could have fallen asleep myself, right where I was. I did not care who won, and in fact I never knew who won.

I am an exhibitor of reptiles. It's in my blood. My father was in the same line of business, and so was my grandfather. From early childhood, all I ever thought about was reptiles. I ate and slept reptiles. Even in late adulthood, all of my dreams contain at least one reptile. That's why I'm in this business. Twelve months out of the year I crisscross this thin, long country of ours to show off my reptile collection. At each town I pitch my lovely tent on a dusty plot of land, then plaster all the surrounding walls with my posters. Even if you have never seen my fabulous show, you have no doubt noticed my beautiful posters? Suitable for framing, they are printed on real cardboard, in four colors, and will not fade. There are those who have accused me of false advertising. They like to kvetch that my snakes always appear much longer on paper than in person. That my salamanders are not nearly as colorful or exotic up close. And that my illustrated alligators, computer-enhanced perhaps, seem primeval, ferocious, while the actual alligators in the show are obviously drugged, passive, and practically made out of rubber. If you flip one over, you can clearly see, in the tiniest print, the always pathetic words "Made in China." There are others who carp that my exhibition includes no two-headed snakes or dragons or a viper that devours its own tail. I cannot waste my time on these people. My critics are obviously only frustrated exhibitors of reptiles. Though they complain, they are always among the first to purchase tickets when my show arrives in town. From inside my booth, I can clearly see them coming from afar, now running, now walking, their faces glowing with a childish excitement. Often they knock real children out of the way to be the very first in line. And yet I do not gloat. Calmly, I can dispense tickets to my enemies without even a smirk on my face. It's no mystery why the whole world is so eager to see my reptiles. Where else, let me ask you, can you and your children learn everything there is to know about this poisonous universe? Where even the most insensate and shell-shocked among you can experience such a rare, lost emotion as revulsion mixed with longing and pity?

# Two Kings

In 1923, my first year in Paris, I was riding the metro from Porte
Maillot to Epinet when I saw a Vietnamese I recognized immediately
as King Khai Dinh. He is remembered nowadays only for the tasteless
concrete tomb he had built for himself. When I saw him, the king
was very thin, yet flabby, with loose folds everywhere. The color of his
face was between yellow and gray, like a rotting lemon. Years in exile
had given him that withdrawn, haunted look. He appeared to be the
sort of aristocrat who would eat opium once a day, play tennis once
a week, and swim in the ocean once a year. On his delicate, match-
stick wrist, the wrist of a princess, was a large square watch, a cheap
LeCoultre, a fact which shamed and saddened me considerably, but
there were no rings on his skeletal fingers. A little odd, I thought, for
a man with so many wives . . . He did not look at anyone or anything
around him but stared straight ahead for a long time. He did not blink
for so long I thought maybe he had gone blind. Swirling in his mind,
no doubt, were confused thoughts about his sad country. He had to
know that history would judge his legacy very darkly. This man was
no more than a puppet king, jerked up and down by a foreign master,
and yet I felt a certain tenderness, even reverence, toward him. His
fate was my fate. I finally got up from my seat to approach my king:
"Your Majesty! You must be King Khai Dinh." His eyes lit up with
the deepest pleasure for a brief moment, but then he responded to
me in French: "Je suis desole, mais je ne comprends pas!" Imagine!

Here was the king of Vietnam feigning ignorance of the Vietnamese language! His French was worse than terrible, however. He spoke with a thick Central accent that gave his origin away immediately. Was the king's bad command of French a conscious act of resistance against his warped identity? One must remember that King Khai Dinh was only ranked as a captain in the French army. I had no time to parse this man's psyche, however. I stared down at his coiled form contemptuously. Jabbed by my disgust, defiance reddened his face, and he flashed me a sarcastic smile. I didn't want to make a scene, however, by having two Vietnamese in badly cut suits shout at each other in front of bemused Frenchmen, so I went back to my seat. I felt so ashamed I actually had tears in my eyes. It wasn't until years later that I found out, through news photographs, that the man I had met on the metro was not King Khai Dinh but Nguyen Ai Quoc.

# My Grandfather the Exceptional

This is a true story about my grandfather: He walked a thousand miles from his native village. He did not intend to go that far. He had wanted to walk maybe one, at most two miles, but, before he knew it, he had walked a thousand miles from his native village. After every mile there appeared a new village, each one utterly different from any place he had seen before. At each village he settled down until they either threatened or politely asked him to move on. He would work at whatever job was available. He was, at various times, a barber, a woodcutter, a sculptor, a slave, a moneylender, a beggar, a politician, a policeman, a thief. He learnt new customs, new slang, new ways of standing up, of sitting on a chair, of sneezing, of scratching his nose. He got new haircuts. Without being aware of it, he learnt to dissimulate his true likes and dislikes. He became overeager to please. He also became hyper-conscious of every single detail of his increasingly abnormal body. He accrued many unpleasant nicknames. Occasionally he would fall in love, be rejected, reject in turn, propose, get married, father children, legitimate and illegitimate, divorce, then reconcile. Once he was drafted into an army and fought bravely against an enemy whom he half suspected to be men from his original village. (He was captured by these enemies, then repatriated in a prisoner exchange.) At another village he was anointed a poet laureate although he could not speak the local language. Finally, at his last village, he looked around and was relieved to find out he was no longer exceptional. Because all old men look alike, disgusted and disgusting, he was finally welcomed into the fraternity of those waiting to die.